THE LOST WHALE

Books by Hannah Gold

THE LAST BEAR

THE LOST WHALE

THE LOST WHALE

HANNAH GOLD

Illustrated by Levi Pinfold

HarperCollins *Children's Books*

First published in the United Kingdom by
HarperCollins *Children's Books* in 2022
Published in this paperback edition in 2023
HarperCollins *Children's Books* is a division of HarperCollins*Publishers* Ltd
1 London Bridge Street
London SE1 9GF

www.harpercollins.co.uk

HarperCollins*Publishers*
Macken House, 39/40 Mayor Street Upper
Dublin 1, D01 C9W8, Ireland

1

PAPERBACK ISBN 978-0-00-841296-8

Hannah Gold and Levi Pinfold assert the moral right to be identified
as the author and illustrator of the work respectively.

Typeset in Aldus LT Std 12pt/21pt

Printed and bound in the UK using 100% renewable electricity at CPI Group (UK) Ltd

A CIP catalogue record for this title is available from the British Library.

This book is produced from independently certified FSC™ paper
to ensure responsible forest management.

For more information visit: www.harpercollins.co.uk/green

To Chris, my ocean and my world

CHAPTER ONE

Arrival

THE FIRST THING Rio Turner noticed when he stepped into the arrivals hall of Los Angeles International Airport was the noise. Airports were never destined to be quiet places and this gigantic, sprawling monster was like a football stadium in full roar.

The second thing he noticed was his grandmother.

Even though it had been five years since he'd last seen her, Rio noticed her straight away. She towered over everyone in a shiny turquoise jumpsuit, wore thick black-rimmed glasses and had a shock of white, wiry hair.

Gazing around, it took a few moments for her to register him. 'Rio?' she asked. 'It is you, isn't it?' She paused in front of him. 'I barely recognised you. You're so . . .'

Her voice tailed off and Rio wondered what she'd been about to say. Either way, he wasn't going to ask. Instead, he crossed his arms protectively against his chest.

'You made it then.' She hurried on, her eyes full of something he didn't recognise. 'I am *so* glad you're here.'

Then she enveloped him in a hug. Not the kind of hug he was used to – deep, warm and snuggly. It was all hard angles and sharp elbows and smelled of peppermints. Rio counted to three before he could bear it no longer. Then he yanked himself away.

'Rio?' she asked falteringly, two bright spots of colour on her cheeks. 'It's been a long time, and I know all this must seem impossibly strange to you right now, but I want you to feel at home while you're staying with me. I am your grandmother after all.'

Rio, who had been staring at the floor during the latter part of her speech, looked up in surprise. She had signed Christmas and birthday cards from Grandma, but he couldn't think of anyone who looked less like a grandmother than her. Not compared to his other grandma anyway, who wore thick, rubber-soled slippers and loved to call him 'ducky' even though the last time he'd checked he hadn't yet grown a beak and feathers. No, this person didn't feel like a grandmother at all, and he secretly resolved to call her by her first name, Fran, instead.

When he didn't answer, she rubbed her hands together despite the fact it wasn't cold. 'Well, I guess we'd better make a move.'

Refusing her offer to carry his case – he was perfectly

capable of that himself – Rio followed her towards the exit where, in the parking zone, she halted by a 4x4 covered in a thick coating of dust.

He climbed into the passenger seat, pulled his seatbelt across and chewed his lip, trying to ignore the sudden, desperate urge for a wee.

As if sensing his discomfort, Fran turned to face him and seemed about to say something. But again, whatever it was died on her lips. Instead, she just cleared her throat. 'I'm . . . sorry about your mother.'

Rio felt the sudden hot sting of tears and rubbed his eyes furiously, hoping she hadn't seen. To avoid any further conversation, he pointedly stared out of the window and, after a brief pause, she switched on the engine with a rough twist of the key, and they were off.

California was the place where Rio's mother had been born and grew up. She'd left when she was barely twenty, first on a music scholarship to New York and then, upon graduation, as a violinist in the London Philharmonic

Orchestra. In all that time, she'd only been back once, taking Rio with her when he was just a tiny baby.

So long ago, he couldn't remember any of it.

But technically, by virtue of his mother's birth, he was half American. Although it was a very small half because he'd lived in London all eleven-and-a-quarter years of his life and spoke with a decidedly English accent. And so this exotic, faraway world of endless sunshine, tall, fluttering palm trees and golden beaches had always felt like a dream. And in truth, Rio had been looking forward to coming back nearly all his life.

Just not like this.

Opening the car window, he took a deep gulp of the Californian air. Unfortunately, this wasn't the cleverest thing to do on a motorway. Rio coughed and spluttered and felt the smog on his lungs.

This was California? Everything was so *big* here. The cars, the road signs, the buildings – even the sky, looping above their heads in a vast indigo silence. As if the car had been picked up and thrown into a world full of giants. London was a city, but it didn't feel anything like *this*.

Mum had always said that California was different. That it was peaceful. That its temperament would suit Rio. That . . .

He closed the window with a snap. Then, ignoring his grandmother's attempts at conversation, he shut his eyes and tried to pretend he was still in a universe where his mother hadn't sent him away to the other side of the world to stay with someone he barely even knew.

CHAPTER TWO

Ocean Bay

A$_T$ SOME POINT, Rio must have fallen asleep because the next thing he knew the car had ground to a halt. 'We're here,' his grandmother said. 'Welcome to Ocean Bay.'

Dusk had stolen in and he had to blink a few times to make sure he was seeing properly. The small coastal town of Ocean Bay was about an hour north of LA. Not that he could spot the town right now. His grandmother lived on the outskirts and the moon shone down on a huge, rambling beach house made of wood. It was a higgledy-piggledy-shaped building three storeys high and painted top to toe in a soft pastel green. In its presence, Rio felt his insides soften. As if the house had magic healing properties and could smooth away even the most jagged of edges.

He rubbed his eyes. The flat he shared with his mother was so small it could probably squeeze itself into this house half a dozen times over.

'It's beautiful, isn't it?' Fran murmured, a note of pride in her voice.

But if he thought the house was special, when Rio stepped out of the car the noise was something else entirely. A magnificent, almighty roar. The kind of noise only something extraordinarily powerful could make.

It was the roar of the ocean.

And Rio, who didn't even like loud noises, discovered to his surprise that this noise was different. He could feel the force of it coursing through his body and had a sudden intense desire to suck the feeling right down into his belly and dislodge the tight band of pain trapped in his chest.

'Plenty of time for you to explore the beach.' Fran beckoned to him from the front step. 'Come inside for now.'

He reluctantly followed her through the wide hallway and into the kitchen, where, unlike back home, there were no photos, school drawings or shopping lists tacked untidily to the wall. There weren't even any dirty mugs or discarded plates or half-eaten ginger biscuits. Instead, the room was full of cool steel appliances that gleamed so brightly he could see his reflection in them – a thin, pale-faced boy with a guarded expression and a thatch of unruly light brown hair that never looked neat, no matter how much he brushed it. The only sign of colour was his favourite yellow T-shirt – the one Mum had bought him for his last birthday.

After a few moments, Fran placed a steaming plate of

food in front of him. 'Vegetable chilli. I made it earlier from my own secret recipe. Eat up now.'

'Th-th-thank you,' Rio replied, hating the way his voice wobbled whenever he felt nervous. The only things he knew about his grandmother were that she was once a head teacher, she'd lived in Ocean Bay all her life and that she spoke with an American accent.

As he ate, she chattered away from the other side of the kitchen. 'I thought tomorrow I could give you a tour of Ocean Bay,' she said. 'Maybe we can go shopping or, or . . . perhaps I could show you the marina or even take you to the lighthouse! Up there, you can see for miles and miles. It's quite the sight. Or, if you're feeling tired, we could just take a walk along the beach together?'

She looked expectantly at him over her glasses.

The words Rio really wanted to say remained stuck in his throat. That he hadn't come here to have fun or go shopping and he most definitely hadn't come here to spend time with someone who hadn't even been part of his life when he'd needed her the most.

Luckily, his grandmother was distracted by the entrance of a long-haired white cat with a black patch of fur over its left eye who announced its presence with a plaintive meow.

'Pirate! There you are! Would you like to meet our guest?'

The cat didn't seem particularly bothered about getting to know Rio, but nevertheless something in his chest softened. He'd always wanted a pet – even if just a hamster – but the apartment rules had forbidden it. He leaned down to stroke the cat behind its ears and was rewarded with a loud purr.

'This is my grandson, Rio. He's come all the way from London to stay with us for a vacation. Do you want to say hello?'

Rio wasn't sure if it was the silly voice she used to speak to Pirate – the kind grown-ups put on for babies – or the fact that he was exhausted after a twelve-hour plane journey, or how she used the American word for holiday. Maybe it was everything. Either way, the words burst out of his chest before he could stop them. 'It's not a *vacation*! I'm not here for fun! I'm only here because I have to be!'

Fran opened and then closed her mouth. Rio thought she was going to say something, but she just shooed Pirate off the table and then busied herself with removing strands of white fur from her jumpsuit.

The rest of the meal passed in silence.

When it was time for bed, Rio followed his grandmother up a flight of rickety wooden stairs, where even through the walls, he could hear the ocean. After pointing out the main bathroom – which had the hugest shower he'd ever seen and could probably fit at least two elephants – she led him up some more stairs to the very top of the house.

'Here's your room,' she said, pushing open the door.

It was a large, vaulted attic space and Rio's eyes immediately feasted on the double bed – much larger than his own tiny bed back home. There was a

21

rectangular-shaped window, hidden by dark blue vertical blinds and the space smelled clean and fresh and ever so slightly of disinfectant.

It was a peaceful room, he decided instinctively. It had a warm, comforting, familiar feel. And there wasn't a single car, bus or motorbike noise. All he could hear was the wash of the sea.

Expecting his grandmother to just disappear, he was surprised to notice she was still there, hovering indecisively in the doorway. Rio placed his case on the bed. Snapping open the clasp, he recoiled from the scent of ginger that wafted out from the biscuits Mum had packed. The smell of them so sharp in the air it almost took his breath away.

'This was *her* room, you know.'

'What?!' He spun round. 'This was my *mum's* room?'

His grandmother nodded. 'She used to practise her violin for hours just standing there. In front of the window. You can still see the grooves of her feet on the floorboards.'

Rio glanced to where she was pointing. To a slightly darkened, furrowed patch where the grain was noticeably more worn than the surrounding boards and where, if you looked hard enough, you could just about make out the outline of a pair of feet.

Without stopping to think, he moved across, carefully placing his own feet where his mother's had been all those years before. Because she was so petite, it was a perfect match. The wood felt warm under his toes. And something else too. Something raw and alive. Standing there in her footprints, it was as if he could feel her music coursing up from the soul of the house where it had been hiding all these years.

Rio closed his eyes and it was as if his mother were there, right in front of him, holding her violin against her neck, her eyes lit up as—

'I'm . . . I'm sorry things have turned out the way they have,' Fran said, faltering. At the sound of her voice, his neck and shoulders stiffened, and the music abruptly faded. 'But she's in the right place.'

'Sh-sh-she's going to get better!' Rio retorted angrily. 'I'll be back home in four weeks and . . . and you'll see! Everything will be normal again!'

Fran opened her mouth to say something but then seemed to decide against it. 'Sleep well then. I'll see you in the morning.'

CHAPTER THREE

Mum

IT WAS EXACTLY one month ago when Rio found out he was being sent to California. It was a Tuesday evening in December and he'd been sitting next to his mum on the sofa while they watched a documentary about polar bears in the Arctic. They were sharing two thick, gooey slices of chocolate cake dished up inside an empty violin case along with a pot of tea.

'Rio-cat,' she said tentatively. This was her special name for him because his ears were ever so slightly pointy at the tips. 'I-I-I have something to tell you.'

'Mmmmm,' he answered distractedly, wondering if she'd let him eat the last bit of cake even though he'd eaten almost all of her slice already.

'I have to go away for a bit,' she said so quietly that Rio thought he'd misheard.

'Go away?' He turned to her in surprise. He couldn't even remember the last time they'd left London. '*Where?*'

Mum tucked a stray strand of red hair behind her ear and swallowed nervously. Her face was alarmingly flushed. 'A . . . hospital.'

Rio's throat tightened so much he could barely breathe. He looked at her aghast.

'A hospital? W-w-what kind of hospital?'

'A special one.' His mother sighed, wiped some crumbs from his chin and explained how some hospitals weren't just for people with physical illnesses. Some hospitals were for people who needed help in other, more invisible ways.

'The doctor says if I don't go . . .'

Rio gulped and his eyes darted around wildly. Anything but look at his mum's face with her crooked smile and too-bright eyes.

But then it got worse. She explained that he was going to stay with his grandmother for four weeks. His father was out of the question because of the new baby, and his paternal grandmother lived in a tiny one-bedroom cottage so that ruled her out too.

'Four *weeks*!' he cried, something rushing so fast in his stomach he felt sick. 'But you hardly ever speak to her!'

'That's because your grandmother and I are two very different people, and the last time we saw each other in London . . . well, we disagreed about a few things.'

'Then why are you sending me there?!'

'It's the best place for you, Rio-cat. The *healthiest*

place. Sometimes you need to put aside your own differences to do the right thing,' she answered tiredly. 'Besides, it's only while I . . . while I get better.'

There was a silence that hung in the air. The kind of silence that comes just before Big Moments. It was, as Rio knew, the worst kind of all.

Mum had always been unpredictable and changeable – sometimes as light and floaty as a flute and other times as sad and heavy as a clash of drums. Rio had thought all grown-ups were like that – until his father informed him that his mum was *different*. When he had pressed his father to find out exactly what 'different' meant, his dad just said that Mum wasn't right in the head. But what did this even mean?

The dark spells often sprang from nowhere, striking at unexpected times and then lingering for days, weeks and in the case of the latest patch, months. This time she'd even taken sick leave from the orchestra – something she had never done before. And even though autumn had been full of golden bronze colours and crisp blue skies, Mum had spent each day locked inside the flat as if she was suddenly afraid of the outside world.

The outside world, as far as Rio could tell, hadn't changed.

But Mum had.

He never knew quite what to expect when he got home from school. Sometimes she wouldn't even be dressed or, if she was, she'd be sitting on the sofa with the curtains tightly drawn. Her favourite peacock-coloured silk scarf – the one she usually only ever wore for concerts – was often stained with splodges of tea. Lately, there'd been a musty, sour smell in the flat that, no matter how many windows he opened, never seemed to go away. And he couldn't even remember the last time she'd cooked a proper dinner.

But to be sent all the way to California? *Alone?*

He took one last look around him as if to drink in his surroundings – the bookshelves crammed with the biographies Mum liked to read, the wobbly music stand by the window, the photos on the mantelpiece of the pair of them at the beach on his seventh birthday – and then finally to his mother. And when he did, he realised he barely recognised her. Her face was wild and loose and ever so slightly scary.

'But . . . but why can't I come with you?'

'Oh, Rio,' she said. 'The hospital's not a place for children.'

'You said yourself how grown-up I am!'

'*Too* grown-up,' she replied gently. 'And you shouldn't be. You should be out there playing, like any other eleven-year-old boy. Not stuck in here looking after me.'

'But I *like* looking after you!' he cried. 'What if I don't want to go all the way to America?'

The thought of being separated from her made him feel bare and exposed as if someone had ripped off a thick overcoat he hadn't even known he'd been wearing. He shivered even though the heating was turned up full blast.

Mum sighed and pinched the bridge of her nose with her fingers. 'The hospital is a place for grown-ups like *me* . . . who need help.'

Rio wanted to protest. To keep protesting until she changed her mind.

But his mum had just started crying. Horrible, ugly tears that fell into her teacup and spilled over the edges. And even though it frightened him when she was like this, Rio took her hand in his. It was a warm, calloused hand from playing the violin, but it was also the softest hand he knew.

And Rio, who had never considered himself particularly brave, took the biggest, boldest breath of his life.

'Okay,' he said in a small voice. 'I'll go.'

And as we had never come across him before, naturally he was took the bravest bird of us all ... lift ... Okay,' he said in a small voice, 'I'll do ...

CHAPTER FOUR

The Phone Call

Rio thought it would take ages to drop off but in fact he tumbled into a sleep so deep and vast it was like he had sunk to the furthest depths of the ocean. A murky, indistinct place of shadows and strange, mysterious sounds that coiled round him. When he finally woke up, it was as if he'd had to take a submarine journey just to reach the surface.

As daylight peeped in through the blinds, he was confused. The bed was far softer than his bed back home. The air cleaner. And the noise. That didn't sound like the hum of traffic.

The Pacific Ocean!

The biggest ocean on the whole planet – an area so vast it was greater than all the continents combined.

Rio flung himself out of bed and rushed to the window, ripped open the blinds and then gasped.

In the bleached light of the bright day, it was dazzling. A patchwork of blue, emerald and turquoise with white horses dancing like diamonds on the surface. The water stretched out forever until it melted into the sky – so you couldn't tell where one ended and the other started. Something light and fizzy rushed through Rio's veins, pushing the last bits of sleep out of his body. Then, as if sensing something coming up through the floorboards, he looked down. And immediately the bubbly feeling vanished.

'*Mum*,' he whispered as a wave of homesickness hit him hard in the chest.

He picked up his mobile phone even though she'd explained she wouldn't be able to send messages. Not because she didn't *want* to. The doctor thought it best if she had a complete break. A break from what though? From *him*? Sometimes, in his darkest thoughts, Rio wondered if all this was his fault.

Instead of using her mobile, Mum would ring on Fran's landline every Sunday, which, due to the time difference, worked out as teatime in London.

A little of the fizzy feeling returned. The first phone call was today!

'Ah, there you are!' Fran smiled tentatively at Rio as he entered the kitchen. 'Did you sleep well?'

Rio nodded, taking in the morning scene where the smell of fresh coffee filled the air and Pirate was stretched out lazily in a patch of sunlight.

'That's the ocean for you. Best medicine in the world.'

She paused. 'I don't know what you normally eat for breakfast, but I can make pancakes, waffles or eggs. What do you prefer?'

'I-I-I . . .' His voice tailed off. Normally, all he ate was a bowl of cereal. Sometimes, if there was no milk, he would eat it dry. But these weren't things Rio liked to talk about.

'Tell you what!' Fran said, mistaking his silence for indecision. 'Why don't I make *all* of them and then you can decide?'

Rio raised his eyebrows. *All of them?*

Without waiting for his answer, she plucked a frying pan from the cupboard, rolled the sleeves of her green jumpsuit up to the elbows and was pulling various cooking implements out of drawers when the phone rang.

The noise was so sudden and shrill that Pirate jumped into the air with shock.

Fran answered and, after a few words, she handed it over. It was all Rio could do not to snatch the receiver off her.

'Hello, Rio-cat,' Mum whispered down the phone.

From the other side of the kitchen, Fran was busy whisking batter, so Rio headed to the back door where, outside, the sky was bright blue with a yellow ball slung high, much brighter and fiercer than the weak sunshine back home. Hard to believe that yesterday he had woken up in the thick of winter.

He sat on the steps and listened to his mother's familiar voice wash over him as she chattered on about her first day in the hospital – which she called a clinic – and what she'd been doing. It was comforting in the way that sometimes rain is comforting. When all you want to do is stay indoors, curl up and watch movies.

'I wish I was there with you,' he murmured, swallowing the lump in his throat.

'It's only four weeks,' she said. 'It'll be gone in no time and, when I see you next, you can tell me all about the things you've been up to.'

Like what? he wanted to say. What exactly was there

to do in Ocean Bay for four whole weeks? But of course he didn't say that.

'How's your grandmother?'

He sneaked a look through the back door where Fran was stirring something on the stove. There were many things he wanted to say, but in the end he chose the simplest.

'She's not you.'

'That's probably a good thing,' Mum answered in a sad voice. 'Rio-cat?'

'Yes,' he replied, biting his lip and feeling helpless.

'I have to go soon, but will you do me a favour?' she asked. 'Hold the phone up so I can hear the ocean. It's been so long since I've been back . . . I want to close my eyes and imagine I'm there with you.'

Rio scrambled to his feet. This was something he could do. 'Hold on!'

He headed to the shoreline, as far as he could go without losing signal, where the sound of the crashing, roaring ocean filled the air like a crack of thunder.

'CAN YOU HEAR IT?'

There was a tiny pause. Rio held the phone up closer to the waves. In and out they pushed. *In and out.*

'I can,' she murmured. 'Oh, I can't tell you how happy that sound makes me.'

When he put the phone back to his ear, Rio could have sworn he heard Mum smiling.

Then she yawned loudly.

'Mum?' He gripped the phone tighter. He wasn't ready to say goodbye. Not yet.

'Yes, Rio-cat?'

'Y-y-you are going to get better, aren't you?'

She let out a long, deep sigh. Not a nice, content sigh but the other kind. Then she said she had to go. Rio stared hard at the ocean where he could see a huge cruise ship far out to sea, sailing further and further away from him.

'Goodbye,' he whispered.

He sat there for the longest of times until the back door opened and the smell of waffles, warm pancakes and fried eggs wafted out.

'Breakfast is ready!' called Fran.

But Rio didn't move. There was no way he could eat anything now. Instead, he curled his knees into his chest and wished with all his heart that he could hear Mum smile once more.

CHAPTER FIVE

Box of Joy

DESPITE THE WARM Californian sun, over the next few days, Rio hung out mostly in his bedroom. Fran offered to show him round Ocean Bay more than once, but each time he found an excuse not to go. Maybe this way she would finally get the message.

He even started marking off the days on a makeshift

41

calendar he had created. Another day gone. One more day closer to talking to Mum again. Another day closer to going home.

But, in spite of this, the time still dragged. Nights were the worst. He would wake up with a clawing feeling in his belly that, no matter how much he tossed and turned, never seemed to go away. Sometimes so ferocious he couldn't breathe.

Come Thursday, Rio was standing in his mum's footprints, trying desperately to conjure her up through the floorboards, when there was a rap on his door.

'Knock knock!' Fran called out. Why she had to say the words rather than just knock, he had no idea. It was just another one of her annoying habits.

'Come in!' he yelled.

'Got your clean clothes for you,' she said, poking her head round the door.

Rio knew he ought to be grateful. After all, he was used to doing his own laundry in London, but somehow the 'thank you' got stuck in his throat. Instead, he picked up his yellow T-shirt and held it close to his face. With a pang, he realised it no longer smelled of home.

Fran put the rest of his clothes down on the bed with a sigh and gave him one of those funny over-her-glasses looks she was fond of. Then she cleared her throat pointedly.

'I know this is not the easiest of times for you,' she said, her cheeks slightly flushed, 'but I'm sure your mom wouldn't want you to spend all your time locked away.'

Rio flinched. When would she get that he didn't want to talk about his mother? Not to anyone. And especially not to her.

'I . . . I thought you might like this?'

He heard her leave the room and then re-enter, placing something on the bed beside him. Something that made the bedcovers dip ever so gently under its weight. Rio kept his eyes pinned on the ocean, so hard his vision blurred, and it wasn't until the door had closed that he bothered to look.

It was a shoebox. Why had she left him a *shoebox*?

And then he noticed the small label in the top right-hand corner with handwriting that was like a punch to the heart.

My Box of Joy

'Mum?' Rio whispered, something hard and brittle snapping deep within him.

He trailed his fingers over the lid. As far back as he could remember, Mum had always collected things that made her smile.

Never expensive things. Not gold rings or fancy trinkets. Simple things. A train ticket from the time they'd been to the beach, heart-shaped pebbles because Mum said hearts made from nature were the best kind of all, a white angel's feather and seashells in which you could hear the ocean from miles and miles away.

She said she collected them because they reminded her to be happy.

He hadn't quite understood it at the time. Why did anyone need reminding to be happy? Surely it was as natural as breathing? But Mum had said being happy wasn't as easy for some people as it was for others. And so, over time, Rio had grown to love collecting things for her. Anything to stop her being so sad.

It took a few moments for him to open the box. First, he popped his fingers under the lid. Then he prised one side up before carefully removing it altogether. The shoebox was crammed full of various ornaments, papers and even an old silk scarf, which, when Rio pressed it to his nose, had the faintest tang of Mum's jasmine perfume still caught in the fibres.

Item by item, he pulled everything from the box and laid it all out on the bed around him. An old report card from school saying that Bella showed remarkable musical ability for someone her age. A receipt for her very first violin. Various birthday cards. The acceptance letter from the music school in New York. A photo of Mum on a boat with windswept hair and the biggest grin Rio had ever seen. Even a boat ticket.

There was one last item at the bottom. An A4

sketchbook. He knew Mum liked to draw in her spare time. Next-door's sausage dog, the cheeky robin that sometimes came to their kitchen window – as well as countless pictures of Rio. But what had she drawn when she was younger? He tentatively turned the first page . . .

The sketchbook was full of whales.

Chapter Six

Grey Whales

Absolutely *full* of them. A head. A tail flicking out of the ocean. Water shooting up from a blowhole. A picture of a whale leaping in the air. Yet another with a whale gliding along the surface. Other sketches capturing more tails, more spectacular leaps, more heads poking out of the water. Some were of

individual whales and others were of mothers and their calves.

Tearing his gaze away, Rio glanced out of the window towards the ocean where the surface lay flat and calm. He remembered Mum telling him about the whales when she was trying to get him excited about California. Apparently, there were lots of them out there. Ones as big as football pitches. Ones with hearts as large as a car. Ones that swam up and down the Californian coastline every year.

'This is the best time of year to visit,' she had exclaimed. 'The grey whales will be passing Ocean Bay on their annual migration south. You'll even get to see one!'

He could still remember the note of excitement in her voice, as if seeing a whale was somehow the best possible thing on earth – better than ice cream or rollercoasters or even birthdays. Rio had doubted seeing a whale could be *that* exciting, but now, looking at the pictures, a strange, shivery feeling ran down his spine.

'You're beautiful,' he murmured, touching the paper gently with his fingertips.

Then, slowly, Rio went through the sketchbook page by page. While all the pictures were spectacular, there was one that stood out.

It was a pencilled drawing of a whale with its head peering up out of the waves. The eye was so vivid that Rio half expected it to blink. He leaned closer to get a better look, and then he put his own eye as close as he could.

It took him a while to place what was so unsettling about the whale's expression. And then he got it. Because it wasn't a wild-animal look at all. It was, Rio realised with a start, a peculiarly human look.

He was about to pull back from the picture when he noticed there was something else in the corner. Handwriting. It was faded, but he was just about able to read it.

White Beak

As Rio peered through the rest of the sketchbook, he noticed that at least ten of the pictures were of the same whale. Each of them drawn with the same love, careful attention but, most of all, the same unbridled joy.

'What's so special about you?' he said gently. 'Who are you, White Beak?'

There was only one way to find out.

Rather than replace the sketchbook in the shoebox, Rio gently cut away the main picture of White Beak and tucked it inside his shorts pocket. It was a chain to his mother – one that covered time and space – and, in some strange, unexpected way, was surprisingly comforting.

Then he rushed down the stairs and through the kitchen. So fast he barely had time to acknowledge Fran on his way out of the back door where the bright Californian sun reflected off the surface of the ocean in a million different shards of light.

Kicking off his trainers, he ran across the warm sand towards the shoreline, which was empty save for a couple of teenage girls carrying surfboards. Here the sound of the ocean drowned out everything – including his own thoughts. A rolling, thundering pounding that filled his ears, followed by a clawing, gnashing, sucking sound as the waves were dragged back out.

Rio stared at a limitless horizon where there was nothing but rolling blue waves and the occasional white gull skimming the surface of the sea. He let out the breath he didn't even know he'd been holding. Because today it wasn't *just* an ocean. A vast blue plain of shimmering water. It was also home to Mum's whale.

He scanned the horizon left to right and then back again. He wasn't daft. He didn't expect to see a whale suddenly leap out of the water in front of his eyes, let alone see White Beak. For all he knew, the whale was

long dead. Yet the sheer raw desire to see one was so strong that he stared and stared and stared until his eyes smarted. But as hard as he looked, the water stayed calm.

Until . . .
CRASH.
SPLAT.
BOOM.

A large wave came from nowhere, smacking him in the chest with a hard thud, and sent him tumbling face down into the water.

'Aaaargghhh!'

When Rio finally found his feet again – shorts sodden and with a mouth full of wet, gritty sand – his first instinct was to check his pocket for his mum's drawing.

'No,' he muttered. 'Please no!'

But the drawing had gone.

A hard, horrible panic gripped him as he dropped to his knees and gazed frantically around. He couldn't have lost it. Not already!

His fingers scraped through the sand, bumping against various shells and pebbles. But it was useless. It could be anywhere. And, even if he did find it, it would be ruined.

He let out a strangled cry. That's when he heard a faint skittering noise.

Ten metres behind him was a girl about his own age, with tangled blonde hair that looked like it hadn't been brushed since birth. The sunlight glinted off her face and gave it a shiny, luminous tint that glowed with the sheen of outdoors.

The girl didn't say anything. Instead, she just held out her hand. And there, wondrously, *miraculously*, was his mum's picture, neatly folded up into squares – just as Rio had left it. He barely managed to stop himself snatching it from her.

'It fell out of your pocket, up there. It was about to blow off in the wind but I caught it.' She stretched her arm out. 'It *is* yours, isn't it?'

Rio nodded. Then cleared his

throat and stood up awkwardly. 'Yes,' he said at last. 'It's mine.' Then he picked the sketch out of her palm, feeling the warmth of it on his fingertips.

'I didn't look at it by the way, if that's what you're thinking.'

Rio blushed. Because that's exactly what he had been thinking. He looked distrustfully at the girl. But she didn't seem sneery or mean – not like some of his classmates back home. Instead, there was something about the frank openness in her face that made it impossible not to believe her.

'Th-th-thank you,' he said, feeling ashamed of how he had judged her, something Mum had always told him not to do.

'You're not from around here?' the girl asked, noting his accent. 'Where do you come from?'

'London,' he replied, spitting out a few grains of wet sand. 'England.'

'Then you shouldn't go too close to the ocean if you're not used to it.' She frowned at his damp clothes, but not unkindly. 'There's a strong current. You can't see it, but it's there and if you're not careful it'll drag you out to sea.'

'I . . . was . . . just . . .'

Rio found himself tongue-tied. This girl had a self-confidence that he had never seen before in someone his age. It wasn't just the red dungarees that had so many pockets it was impossible to count them all, or the green, short-sleeved T-shirt that matched the colour of her eyes. It was the way she held herself.

Like she owned the entire ocean.

'Do you live here?'

'Over there.' She pointed in the direction of the lighthouse. 'With my dad.' She smiled at the mention of him. The kind of smile that lit up her entire face from the inside out. If Rio had been the envious sort, he might have been jealous of that smile and everything it contained.

'Anyway,' she said, winking at him, 'you know what you need, don't you?'

He shook his head.

'Deeper pockets!'

And, with one last grin, she skipped away.

Chapter Seven

The Museum

'F-F-Fran?' Rio asked once he was back in the kitchen.

She was hunched over the crossword with a pursed brow. Sitting down, she looked much smaller and older somehow. For the first time, he noticed how some of her fingers were swollen with age and he felt that horrible hot flush of shame that comes when you've not been your kindest, best self.

'Yes, Rio?' She put down the pen and turned her attention to him. Her expression was wary and, by her ankles, Pirate stood guard.

'The box . . .' he said, then cleared his throat. His mouth was as dry as a desert. 'The box had a sketchbook in it and I wondered . . . I wondered why . . .'

'Your mother drew so many pictures of the whales?'

Rio nodded gratefully.

Rather than answer, Fran folded up the newspaper and grabbed her car keys.

'I think the best thing to do is for you to change into some dry clothes, and then I'll show you.'

Rio wasn't sure where they were headed, but Fran drove towards the centre of Ocean Bay. Even though he had been in California a few days, it was the first time he'd actually been anywhere other than Fran's house or the patch of sand outside her back door. Stretched along the ocean's edge, it was a small town with a palm-lined avenue running parallel to the beach. There was a wide pedestrian boardwalk filled with runners, walkers, mothers pushing prams, skateboarders, roller-bladers, scooters and even a man dressed in a whale costume riding a unicycle.

'We get a lot of tourists this time of year,' Fran said, following his gaze. 'The grey whales pull people in from all over.'

Before Rio could question her any further, she pulled into a marina where the tall white lighthouse stood protectively over a U-shaped harbour full of various-sized boats bobbing gently in the ocean breeze. She parked by a large, square-fronted building with a hand-painted sign announcing it was the Ocean Bay Museum.

Rio's heart sank. She had brought him to a *museum*?

Heavy-footed, he followed her to the entrance where she pushed open the glass door and ushered him inside. It was a large, cavernous space and lining each wall were floor-to-ceiling glass cabinets. There was also a giftshop with a tiny café adjoining it. But it was what took centre stage that stole Rio's breath away.

Hanging from the ceiling was the full-sized skeleton of a whale.

Parts of it had been suspended using wire, while other sections were propped up from below. It was the biggest skeleton Rio had ever seen. Bigger than a London bus. The jawbones were longer than he was.

'*Eschrichtius robustus*,' Fran said.

Rio wondered if his ears were working properly. His grandmother didn't have a particularly strong American accent, but she now seemed to be speaking in a completely different language altogether.

'Latin,' she explained. 'It means grey whale.'

Rio wanted to ask a thousand and one questions, but somehow they all ended up stuck in his throat.

'You asked about your mother and that sketchbook?' Fran reminded him. 'The Pacific coastline is the major migratory route for the grey whale, which means that around this time every year they pass by Ocean

Bay on their way south to Mexico and then in two to three months, you'll see them returning north again, sometimes with a calf.'

'And my mum?' Rio asked breathlessly. 'She used to watch them?'

'Ah,' his grandmother replied. 'This is what I wanted to show you. See?'

She had taken a couple of steps away and was pointing at some old photographs in one of the free-standing glass cabinets. Rio peered over her shoulder to take a closer look. The photo she was pointing to was of a small boat out on the open water. There were a handful of people onboard . . . including a young girl with red curly hair and a huge grin.

'Mum!' he exclaimed.

Fran nodded. 'Your grandfather took her on that boat trip when she was about seven. Her first-ever one. Oh, I still remember when she came home. Her eyes were like saucers! She'd seen a grey whale swim right past the boat. Said it was the most magical thing she'd ever laid eyes on and that it made her heart smile. After that, she begged us to go every day.'

Rio was still gazing at the photo of his mother. She looked so carefree, so healthy, so *happy*. He wished he could peel open the cabinet and press the photo to his own heart. He was staring at it so hard he didn't realise Fran was still talking.

'But of course we don't get grey whales all year round, only in wintertime. So, for the rest of the year, your mom would come here. Everything you want to know about grey whales is in this museum.'

She was about to say more when someone called her name from the other side of the room. 'Excuse me a moment, Rio, will you?'

He nodded and as she moved away, he noticed that dotted round the skeleton were various handwritten signs in both English and Spanish. They listed facts about the grey whale.

In this way, he soon discovered:

Grey whales are the seventh largest of all the whale species.

There are approximately 20,000—30,000 of them.

They grow in length to about 13—15 metres.

They can live between 55 and 70 years.

They are only found in this part of the world — the Pacific Ocean.

Because of this, they are sometimes also referred to as the Pacific grey whale or even the Californian grey whale.

Fran was still chatting to her friend, so Rio shifted his attention back to the photo of his mum. There were a few other pictures of the boat trip, but no other clear shots of his mother. Apart from one. It was taken from a different angle, presumably by his grandfather, and showed the back of Mum's head as she leaned over the side of the boat.

Where in the water there was a grey whale.

The photo was slightly blurry and there were so many people in the way that Rio couldn't see much of the whale at all. Just a grey smudge. But it was a grey smudge with distinctive white markings on its face.

White Beak.

Chapter Eight

Hunted

Rio pulled the picture of White Beak from his pocket. It was hard to be sure they were the same whale. But if so, surely this explained why his mother had drawn so many pictures of this particular animal.

It had been the first whale Mum had ever seen – the one that had stolen her heart. The one that had put that huge, beaming grin on her face. Rio gazed from the photo to the picture and then back again. Something lit up in his chest. No wonder it was in her Box of Joy.

Suddenly Rio was hungry to find out as much as possible – not just about White Beak but all the grey whales. He turned his focus to the other photos in the glass cabinets. At first, they were just black-and-white historical shots of Ocean Bay, but then there were a few more spectacular ones of the ocean – pods of dolphins leaping out of the water, huge turtles with wizened faces and shoals of silvery fish.

He switched his attention to the final cabinet and immediately wished he hadn't. The first photo was an awful one of a man carrying a harpoon gun and grinning wildly as a dead calf lay on the deck of his ship. A quick glance told Rio that the other photos were all similar.

Ships laden with dead whales, seas of thick red blood, whales cut up into pieces, and all accompanied by smiling people brandishing harpoon guns.

Rio felt sick. Even though it was all many years ago, his throat tightened.

'It gets most people too,' his grandmother said, coming up behind him and standing by his shoulder. 'Seeing them like this.'

'But why would they do that to them?!' Rio asked, turning to her. '*Why?*'

'Back then, people didn't see whales the way we do now,' replied Fran, frowning. 'They were a source of money for the whalers who sold their meat and used the blubber for oil. Even whalebone was a precious commodity. Up until not that long ago, ladies even used to wear whalebone corsets.'

'B-b-but that's not right!' Rio gasped, picturing Mum's whale. 'Humans can't just go around killing them because . . . because they want to *wear* them!'

'Well, we don't any more,' said Fran. 'Not as much anyway.'

'Not as *much*?!' A wave of emotions was tossing and turning in Rio's chest, some so hot and fiery he could barely breathe. 'You mean some people still hunt them?'

Fran pushed her glasses up her nose and gave him a strange, impenetrable look. 'You're so much like your mom when she was your age,' she said with a sigh.

'In what way?'

'She used to get upset about whale hunting too. Even went on a few protest marches,' she replied. 'Though I told her it was a waste of time.'

'Why . . . why was it a waste of time?' he retorted angrily. 'How could saving a whale ever be a waste of time?'

'Because what can one girl do?' Fran shrugged. 'Especially one like her?'

Like her?

'Sometimes I don't even think she was fighting against the hunters,' she continued, rubbing her hands together tiredly. 'She was fighting against herself. Your mother . . . your mom has been—'

CRASH.

Rio swung out a hand. He didn't mean to. He didn't

70

even know he was doing it. Anything just to stop his grandmother talking. His arm shot out, and it banged against one of the glass cabinets next to the skeleton. The one with all the photos of the dead whales. It wobbled and quivered.

For a horrible, brief moment, everything was suspended.

And then *SMASH*.

The cabinet collapsed to the floor, shattering into a thousand different pieces, and photos of whales swam out across the floor.

Fran looked shocked. She had taken off her glasses and was staring at him as if he were a stranger.

'Rio?' she asked in a small, tight voice. 'Are you okay?'

Rio wiped his face, surprised and embarrassed to find he was crying. Before she could say another word, he spun round and sprinted out of the door.

CHAPTER NINE

The Pier

RIO LEFT THE museum and ran and ran until his chest was heaving and he could run no more. Hot waves of shame coursed through him as he pictured his grandmother's face and the mess he'd left behind. At some point later, he would have to face the music.

But not yet.

He ended up on the beach. Even though it was full of children playing volleyball, Rio felt completely alone. They were shrieking with laughter, while in contrast he felt as though he was wearing one of those whalebone corsets, pulled so tight he could barely breathe.

Oh, why had Mum sent him here?

He gazed around frantically as if the answer would materialise out of the bright Californian air. He'd tell his grandmother to put him back on the nearest plane, *beg* her if need be, then he would convince the doctors to let him into the hospital and he would . . .

His thoughts skidded to a stop because what exactly *would* he do if he went back to London? All he'd ever wanted was to make his mother better.

But no matter how fast he had rushed home from school, how many weekend activities he'd given up to be with her, how often he'd cooked dinner or even how tightly he had held his mum's hand – none of that had ever been enough. Rio had looked after her for as far back as he could remember. Long after her friends stopped visiting. But he still hadn't been able to stop her going into hospital.

He had failed.

Without him wanting it to, a sob burst out of his lips and Rio sank on to the nearest bench where he folded himself up into a tiny ball and wished with all his heart that he could go back in time and do things differently. He wished lots of other things too – things he didn't usually like to admit even to himself – that Mum was more like other mothers, and that he had a normal eleven-year-old life. The kind of wish that makes you feel guilty for even thinking it at all.

He didn't know how long he sat curled up there. It might only have been seconds. It might equally have been hours. But after a while, Rio realised he wasn't alone. No one had sat on the bench next to him. It wasn't *that* kind of company.

It was the company of something far more comforting.

It was the ocean. Pushing in and out on the beach. Not just pushing but breathing.

In, out, in, out. In, out, in, out.

And, as it breathed, that's when the idea came. Maybe it was the ocean carrying it to Rio from far out at sea. Maybe it was a voice even deeper than that. Either way, the plan popped into his head as if by magic. He might not have been able to save Mum from going into hospital. But it wasn't too late to save her *now*.

Rio pulled out the picture of White Beak from his pocket.

Because this was part of it.

He would go whale watching and find her some whales.

He would take photos of whales.

He would video whales.

Whale after glorious whale!

And then he'd send them all to Mum. Because surely she would look at her phone at least once? And when she did, she'd have something to make her smile again. Like the way she'd smiled on the boat trips when she was younger. She always said that she needed reminding to be happy. Well, here was the answer! Here was the answer to everything! Because if the whales could make her happy again, then perhaps . . . perhaps she could even get better and she wouldn't have to be stuck in that hospital for too much longer.

The idea shone and glistened in his mind and without even pausing to take another breath, Rio was sprinting back towards the place where he'd noticed a whale-watching tour kiosk earlier. As he careered down the boardwalk, his thoughts spiralled and ran and scampered. So fast he felt giddy trying to catch up.

Finally, he arrived at the kiosk, sweat dripping down the back of his neck and his breath coming out in rattles and rasps. He skidded to a halt.

The kiosk was indeed the place to book whale-watching tours. But not only had the last one left two hours ago, the kiosk was well and truly closed. The next trip was scheduled for tomorrow, and Rio gulped when he saw the price.

It was a lot of money even for just one hour. He had some savings, but they were in a bank account in England. And it wasn't as if he could ask his grandmother. No way could he tell her his plan.

He banged his fists against the kiosk in frustration. His plan was over before it had even begun. Shoulders slumped, he headed back to the museum and tried hard to ignore the lump in his throat.

It was then he caught a flash of red out of the corner of his eye.

A figure was standing partway along the pier, and there was something very familiar about it.

The red dungarees. The wild blonde hair. The way her chin jutted up.

It was the girl from the beach.

She was standing perfectly still, gazing out to sea with a pair of binoculars pressed to her eyes. Once in a while, she paused to write things down in a notebook. Rio couldn't help but be curious and, without even thinking about it, he crept nearer.

He'd got about ten metres away when, as if sensing someone was watching her, the girl spun and looked around her wildly before locking eyes with him. She beckoned him over with quick, fluttery fingers.

'Look!' she said hurriedly, seemingly unsurprised to see him and jabbing her finger excitedly at a point somewhere on the horizon. '*Quick!* You'll miss it.'

She grabbed Rio's shoulder and twisted him round to face the ocean. There was the taste of excitement in the air, so alive he could almost touch it, but no matter how hard he stared into the distance to where the sea merged into the sky, he couldn't see anything apart from a sailing boat, its white sails flapping in the breeze.

'There!' she cried. 'The tail!'

Rio squinted harder. And then. So quick. He almost missed it. The most majestic, ginormous, dark-slicked tail gliding up out of the water and then sliding back under the surface.

'A whale!'

Chapter Ten

Marina

Rio rubbed his eyes in disbelief. He had just spotted a whale. A real-life whale in the wild! Even though it was far away, it was the most incredible thing he had ever seen.

'Was that a grey whale?' he asked excitedly, unable to believe his luck. He'd only just come up with the plan and now look!

The girl nodded. 'You can tell by the shape and size of their fluke – that's their tail. The grey has a much rounder tail than other whales.'

'You can tell the difference even from here?!' Rio spun round to face her incredulously.

'You can if you watch them as much as I do,' she replied, jotting something down in her notebook, which was full of columns of numbers and strange, indecipherable squiggles. 'I'm Marina,' she said, snapping shut the notebook and slipping it back into one of her pockets. 'Marina Silver.'

'Rio,' he said shyly, holding out his hand. 'Rio Turner.'

Marina studied his outstretched hand as if she'd never come across a handshake before. Perhaps she hadn't. Just as Rio was thinking he had made some huge, embarrassing mistake, she reached her own out. Her clasp felt warm and surprisingly rough.

He probably ought to have been heading back to the museum. But somehow his feet didn't move. Instead, he leaned closer.

'Are you whale watching?' he whispered.

He'd never met a whale watcher before. He wasn't even sure what they looked like. But, if he could have imagined one, they probably would have looked like this girl with her wild, sea-spun hair and eyes the colour of a mermaid's tail.

Marina nodded. 'I watch lots of whales, but greys are my favourite.'

Just like Mum! Rio almost said. But then stopped himself. He didn't like talking about his mother to anyone. Not since the time he'd spoken about her to Billy Jenkins at school, who he thought was his friend. But then Billy had told everyone else and they'd all avoided him for weeks as if there was something wrong with *him* too.

'W-w-why do you like the grey whale the best?'

'I prefer animals that are different.' She shrugged.

Different like Mum, Rio thought, his heart squeezing against his chest. 'How do you mean?'

'Lots of people think the grey whale just looks like a crusty old rock because it has all these barnacles on its back and snout,' Marina said, pointing to her own face, which thankfully was barnacle-free. 'But I don't think they're ugly at all. How can a whale *ever* be ugly? They're the most beautiful animals on the planet.'

She looked defiantly at Rio. Perhaps to judge if she had said too much or he might dare to disagree. But of course he didn't think that at all. Instead, his heart gave a funny, squiggly little jump.

'Do you know what people call the grey whale?' she asked, lowering her voice even though no one else was around.

Rio racked his brain to remember what the notice had said in the museum. 'The Pacific whale?'

Marina shook her head. 'The *friendly* whale.'

'But . . . but how can a whale be friendly?'

'Because sometimes on boat trips, the grey whale will actually come right up to the boat like this –' Marina held out her arm – 'and let you *touch* it.'

'No!' Rio had a horrible feeling that she was pulling his leg.

'Ocean's promise,' she said. 'And that's the best promise of all because the ocean is the most powerful thing on earth. Even more powerful than humans. Although most humans don't like to admit that.'

'Have you ever touched one?'

'Just once and it was the best thing ever . . . Like touching a rainbow.'

Rio gazed at Marina in awe.

'My dad runs whale-watching tours,' she continued, her eyes shiny and bright. 'And not just any tours – the *best* whale-watching tours in Ocean Bay.'

'Whale-watching tours?' Rio gasped. 'Your dad?'

If Marina noticed his jaw was hanging open, she didn't comment. 'People come to Ocean Bay from all over the world to see the grey whales. I thought that was why you were here too?'

It was a simple question, but one Rio wasn't sure how to answer. He gazed at her frank, open face, then back out to the ocean.

Slowly, wave by wave, the answer cemented itself

somewhere in his belly. As if it had been there all along. 'Yes,' he replied decisively, looking back at her. 'Yes. I *am* here for the whales.'

Marina nodded. Almost as if there could be no answer other than that one.

'So, what are you waiting for?' She grinned impishly. 'Want to come watch some with me?'

Chapter Eleven

Whale Watching

Two days later, Rio stood waiting. Apparently, Marina's dad was doing some essential boat repairs so watching from the pier was the next best thing. Also Marina said it meant she could train Rio. Although why he needed training just to watch some whales, he had no clue.

No matter. She'd be here soon and then, after today,

he would have so much more to tell Mum when he spoke to her on Sunday.

Rio's heart buzzed and shone in excitement at the thought.

He'd even mellowed slightly towards his grandmother. Mainly because it was hard to keep being cross at someone for so long. Also because he had found her frantically searching the marina when he'd returned the other day. But rather than be angry with him she'd seemed relieved and even slightly emotional that he'd come back. Rio had been the carer for so long that it was a slightly odd feeling to be the one being cared for.

'Oh, Rio,' she'd exclaimed. 'Please don't ever run off like that again.'

Then she'd given him one of her peppermint-smelling hugs.

And, not only did she take him shopping to kit him out with new shorts, sunglasses and ocean-friendly suntan lotion, she'd also lent him her binoculars. Admittedly, they were heavy, clunky things and he'd had to wipe off a couple of cobwebs and a stray spider first.

While he waited on the pier for Marina, he practised using the binoculars to stare at the horizon.

'I like your shorts. Nice deep pockets!'

Rio jumped. He had been so lost in thought, he hadn't heard Marina come up behind him.

'I . . . er . . . took your advice.'

'Anyway, you're looking all wrong. You're waving the binoculars around like they're some kind of pompom.' She grabbed them from his hand and then pointed them at the horizon, holding them perfectly still for the longest of times. 'Like that. You need to keep them focused in one place. The first and most important rule for a whale watcher is patience.'

She held the binoculars out, and Rio took them silently, before realising she expected him, there and then, to resume his watching. Placing them against his eyes, he couldn't help but feel like he was sitting some kind of test. As if on cue, Marina reached out her hand and corrected the height at which he was holding them.

'Angle them more like this. That's it. Now just hold them steady!'

Rio did exactly as she instructed, even when his eyes felt as if they were going to pop out of his head from staring so hard.

'There!' She pointed excitedly to the horizon. 'Three o'clock!'

It took Rio a second to realise Marina wasn't telling him the time, but was actually directing him where to look by using a clock face as a geographical marker. By the time he'd worked that out, all he saw was the faintest splash of water, but no whale.

Even without binoculars, her eyesight was as sharp as an eagle's. But no matter how hard Rio looked all he could see were the white crests of waves breaking, a few brave surfers and the occasional sailing boat.

'The second rule of whale watching,' she said reassuringly, as if sensing his disappointment, 'is never to give up. Now you know where the whale is, move your binoculars a fraction to the left and keep them steady. Wait, wait, wait . . . It will resurface anytime . . . now! See that plume of water?'

If Marina hadn't told him, Rio would have completely missed it. Just a splash gone before he even had time to wonder what it was. It happened so quickly he hadn't even managed to get his phone out, let alone take pictures to send to his mum.

'Was it the whale's tail making that splash?'

'No!' Marina giggled. 'It's their breath!'

'Their *breath*?'

'Whales are more like humans than we think,' she explained. 'They need air just like us and unless they regularly come up to the surface to breathe they drown. So that plume of water you saw is actually the whale breathing out through its blowholes.'

Rio had never stopped to imagine how a whale breathed before. Or even what a whale's breathing looked like. But, then again, his old life hadn't been spent under the dazzling Californian light with the sound of the ocean in his dreams.

After twenty more minutes, in which Marina had spotted one more whale – a humpback apparently – Rio had failed to see any. Worse, his arms had started to ache from holding the binoculars. Marina was right. Whale watching, he was quickly discovering, was a lot harder than it looked.

'Here.' She rummaged in her pockets, pulling out a nailfile, some gum, a biro and then her binoculars – which were a third the size of Rio's. 'You can have these if you want.'

'Are you sure?'

Marina glanced at his binoculars and grimaced. 'Yours must be at least a million years old! Anyway, I've got another pair at home.'

As he put them in his pocket, Rio's fingers touched the edge of his mum's picture and he pulled it out lest the binoculars squash it.

'What is that?' Marina asked curiously. 'It must be very important to you if you carry it around with you all the time.'

Rio cradled the drawing protectively against his chest. 'It's a whale,' he answered, omitting the fact that his mother had drawn it.

She nodded, not in the way that some people nod when they aren't really listening. But as if she knew there was something else he wasn't telling her. He braced himself for the inevitable questions, but instead Marina just smiled.

'Can I look?'

He paused a fraction of a second before handing it over. What harm was there to let her? Besides, if he could show anyone a picture of a whale, it would be this girl.

Marina took the sketch and spread it out in her hands.

'Oh!' she exclaimed with a start. 'It's White Beak.'

Chapter Twelve

The *Spyhopper*

Rio's jaw dropped wide open. 'You *know* White Beak?' he asked in disbelief. He had hardly dared believe the whale would still be alive, let alone that other people might actually know of it. 'B-b-but how?!'

'Come with me,' Marina said, handing back the picture with a wide grin, 'and I'll show you.'

Before Rio could answer, she led him towards the centre of the harbour where boats of all sizes were moored up to wooden jetties – sailing boats with masts that creaked and sighed in the wind, fishing boats with lobster pots stacked high on decks stinking of fish, sleek cruisers with flowery names and boats that had been battered at sea and looked like relics from a bygone era.

Marina skipped along a tiny jetty before finally skidding to a halt about halfway down.

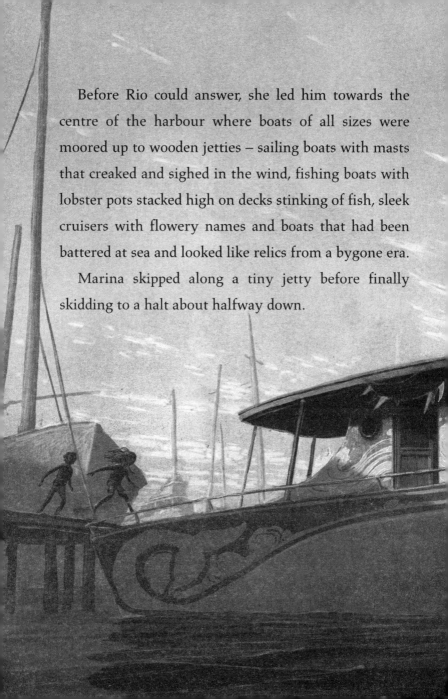

'Here we are,' she said. 'Welcome to my home!'

'*This?*' Rio was unable to hide his shock. When she'd said her dad ran whale-watching tours, he had never imagined she actually lived on the boat too. 'This is where you live?'

'Of course!' she said, giggling. 'Where else would someone called Marina live?!'

The boat in front of them was *anything* but normal.

It had been painted to resemble a grey whale.

The hull was gunmetal grey, with the outline of the whale's body running the length of it. Where the boat tapered off at the rear, someone had sketched in a tail curling round the edge of the boat, and, at the front, a remarkably lifelike eye had been painted on. Finally, fluttering from the deck was a rainbow flag, gently curling in the breeze.

'Isn't she just the best!' Marina exclaimed, clapping her hands together in glee.

Personally, Rio felt it was a little much. But then everything had been brighter, bolder, bigger since he'd arrived in Ocean Bay. It was as if, by being here, someone had dialled up the brightness of his life, and he had to blink to adjust. But, if anything could help him get close to the whales, this boat was most definitely it.

'She's called the *Spyhopper*,' Marina said, pointing at the handwritten lettering on the side of the hull.

'The *Spyhopper*?'

'It's something grey whales do,' she explained, throwing her arms in the air. '*WHOOSH!* They push their heads out of the water like this. Almost as if they're standing up. And then they have a good look around before disappearing again. It's called spyhopping. No one really understands why they do it, but it's one of the reasons why I love them so much.'

'You've brought a guest, I see.'

'Dad!' Marina spun round, giving him a mock captain's salute. 'You don't mind, do you?'

Rio swallowed. Marina's dad wasn't like his – a dad who wore grey suits to work and spent much of his spare time either watching football on the television or playing on his phone. But then Rio wasn't sure what to expect from someone who lived on a boat and ran whale-watching tours for a living. He was older than Rio had anticipated, with thick, unruly hair salted with flecks of silver and whiskers on his cheeks. His face was tanned, with creases round the eyes, and a nose that had been broken at least twice. He was tall, with broad shoulders, and wore cowboy boots and a white shirt under a waistcoat the colour of the sea.

But it was his voice that captivated Rio the most. It was deep, like rich dark chocolate. The kind of voice a double bass would have if it could talk. And, when he spoke, it was as if the earth itself should sit up and listen.

'Please jump onboard.'

Rio had never been on a boat before. The gap between the *Spyhopper* and the wooden jetty was only a step, but it was a step over water nevertheless. And who knew what lay below? Marina jumped across without a second thought and, crossing his fingers for luck after a slight pause, Rio did likewise.

The deck shifted slightly under his feet, as if he hadn't just landed on a boat but a different world. He noted the steering wheel, the sturdy bench seating that wrapped round the inside of the railings and three wooden steps down into the cabin.

'Welcome aboard the *Spyhopper*,' Marina's dad said, holding out a hand that felt strong and bearlike. The kind of hand that could make you feel safe.

'Birch,' he said, introducing himself. 'Wonderful to meet you at last.'

At last? Rio raised an eyebrow.

'Marina hasn't stopped talking about you. You've made quite the impression.'

Rio's insides somersaulted. Marina had been talking about *him*?

Birch smiled and then motioned for them to follow him down into the cabin, which was deceptively large and square. It smelled of coffee and something else Rio couldn't identify – but if he had to put a label on it, he would have said it was the whiff of buried treasure.

The cabin was practically furnished, making use of every spare bit of space. Two cushioned benches faced each other, with a small, secured table separating them, which he guessed folded down to make a double bed, and another two doors that led presumably into another bedroom and a bathroom. On the other side was a kitchenette – although that label was generous. In reality, it was the tiniest of hobs and a fridge. On the wall was a porthole that let in a stream of sunshine, surrounded by various in-built shelves and cubbyholes stuffed with papers, books, shells, nick-nacks and pieces of driftwood carved into ornamental shapes. Tacked on the opposite wall was a map charting the entire Pacific coastline.

'Dad?' said Marina. 'Rio wants to know about White Beak. He's even got a picture of her.'

'*Her?*' Rio asked, although deep down he wasn't surprised that White Beak was female.

Marina nodded. 'We know it's a her because females are slightly larger than males. Show Dad the sketch, won't you?'

Rio fished the drawing out of his pocket and handed it over reluctantly, hating whenever it was out of his grasp. The older man stood for a long time, just staring at it. 'Who drew this? Do you know?'

Rio swallowed nervously. 'My . . . mum.'

'Your mother?' Birch raised his eyebrows as if expecting an explanation.

But Rio merely nodded and then took the picture back. Despite the fact that Marina and her dad were clearly curious, there was no way he was going to tell them about Mum. What if they laughed? Or gave him one of those horrible, pitying stares? Or, worse, no longer wanted him on their boat? Instead, he folded the picture up and placed it carefully back in his pocket.

'I just want to find out as much as I can about White Beak,' he said, hoping that answer would satisfy them.

'Then take a seat, Rio,' Birch replied.

Chapter Thirteen

Happywhale

After putting a saucepan of milk on the stove to heat, Birch pulled a smaller rolled-up map from one of the cubbyholes and spread it out across the table.

'This is the migratory route of the grey whale,' Marina said, helping her father pin down the corners with large conch-shaped shells so it wouldn't curl up again.

Rio couldn't quite see how this was connected to White Beak, but he nodded anyway. He would sit and listen to anything right now if it meant getting closer to Mum's whale.

'At the top here is Alaska,' Birch explained, pointing to the largest state of the US, which actually sat above Canada. 'That's in the Arctic, and that's where the grey whales eat krill that you only find in cold water.'

'Some whales are top feeders, which means they eat their food on the surface of the water. But others, like the grey whales, are bottom feeders. They open their mouth like this –' Marina stretched her mouth wide – 'and then they scrape it along the bottom of the seabed and shovel tonnes of krill in.'

Birch nodded. 'That's a great impression, Marina. You'll make a great whale yet. Although I don't recommend mimicking one at the dinner table anytime soon.'

'After feeding,' Marina continued, purposefully ignoring her dad's teasing, 'the whales swim the entire length of the Pacific coast, from Alaska through to Canada, and then *all* the way down the west coast of America, past Washington, Oregon and California where we are and finally down to the lagoons in Mexico.'

Rio looked at the distance. Even on the map, it seemed an impossibly long way.

'It's a ten- to twelve-thousand-mile round trip,' Marina said as if reading his mind. 'It's one of the longest migration routes of any animal on earth. And no one really knows *how* they even do it – how they manage to find their way and don't get lost or anything. It's like they carry a map of the ocean in their minds. Grey whales are *way* smarter than us, even with all our technology. They do it every single year. There and back.'

'Why?' Rio asked, feeling tired just thinking about it.

'In summer, they need to feed in the Arctic because that's where all the krill is, but come fall they have to travel further south, where it's much warmer, to have their calves.' Birch pointed to three or four bodies of water that looked like estuaries cutting into the coastline of Mexico.

'For thousands of years, that's where the grey whales

have travelled – to these shallow lagoons, which are far safer places for them to give birth than in the open water. Then, when the calves are strong enough, the mothers and the calves will swim all the way back north again.'

At which point, the milk started to bubble. While Birch mixed in the chocolate powder and served up the kind of frothy hot chocolate Rio loved best, Marina removed the notebook – the one with all the strange numbers and squiggles – from her pocket.

'See this? As the grey whales pass by Ocean Bay, we make a note of any we spot.'

'I thought you were just watching them?' Rio asked, confused.

'We are watching,' Marina replied. 'But we're also *counting* them.'

'By noting any grey whales that pass by Ocean Bay on their way to the lagoons, we help keep track of their population,' Birch explained. 'Of course, someone like me, who runs whale-watching tours, can actually be of huge assistance.'

WHALE MIGRATION MAP

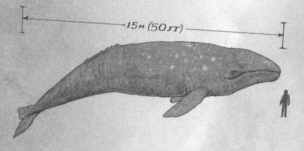

15 m (50 ft)

During their migration, grey whales travel an average of roughly 75 miles (120 km) per day at an average speed of 5 miles per hour (8 kph).

They feed in the cold Arctic waters and calve and mate in the warm, protected tropical lagoons of the Pacific Ocean off Mexico.

In total, this round-trip covers a distance of roughly 12,000 miles (20,000 km) and is believed to be the longest annual migration of any mammal on Earth.

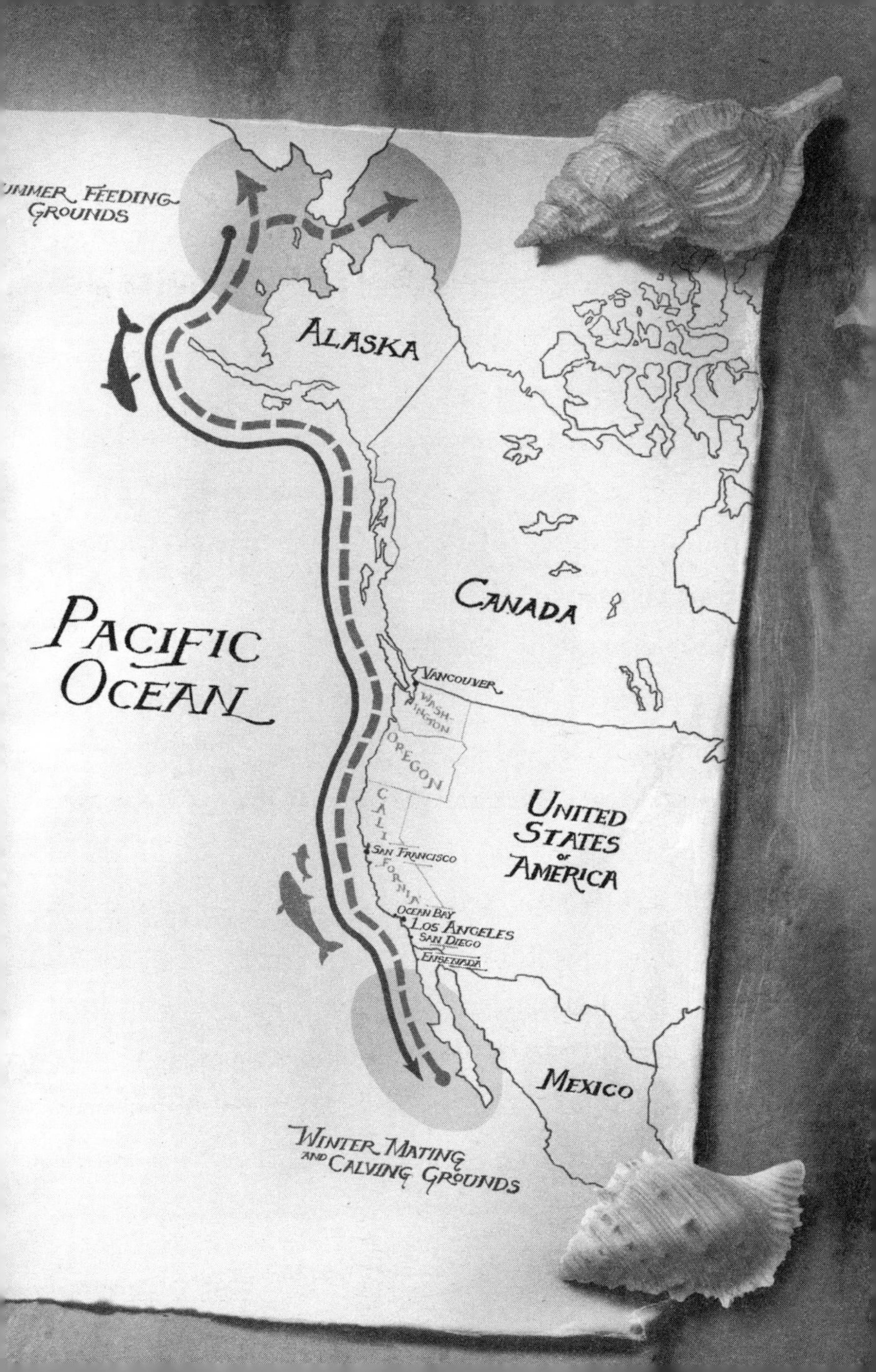

SUMMER FEEDING
GROUNDS

ALASKA

CANADA

PACIFIC
OCEAN

VANCOUVER

WASH-
INGTON

OREGON

CALI-
FORNIA

SAN FRANCISCO

OCEAN BAY
LOS ANGELES
SAN DIEGO
ENSENADA

UNITED
STATES
OF
AMERICA

MEXICO

WINTER MATING
AND CALVING GROUNDS

'Huge assistance to *who*?'

'A marine biologist set up a special whale-counting database about six years ago,' Birch answered. 'Although counting whales might not seem *that* big a deal in the grand scheme of things,' he continued, 'the data collected is incredibly important information for marine biologists, scientists and environmentalists in helping monitor whale populations and understanding any threats they face.'

That made sense. Rio supposed it was no different to the birdwatch they did as a class project every spring – counting all the different types outside his bedroom window. Except this time the animal involved was A LOT bigger.

'I'll show you how it works.' Marina pulled out a laptop from one of the cubbyholes and opened it up to a website called Happywhale. 'The whole point of the database is that *anyone* can join in, no matter how old you are or where you come from,' she said. 'You don't need to be a scientist or anything. All you have to be able to do is spot a grey whale and then upload your sightings to the website – either with a photo or just a description. Now there are thousands of people all along the Pacific coast who count them too!'

Rio thought back to his grandmother's comment about Mum – how one girl can't make a difference. She was wrong. You *can* make a difference when you all work together.

Although one thing was still puzzling him. 'But how can you tell the grey whales apart from the other whales?!'

Marina spat out her drink and it sprayed all over the table. 'Whales don't look and sound exactly the same!' she gasped. 'Watchers can spot the differences with their eyes shut!'

'Perhaps not *shut* exactly,' said Birch. 'But Marina is right. Every whale species has distinctive characteristics – from the size and shape of their fluke, the colour of their skin, the position of the dorsal fin – even the height and shape of their plume can differ widely. All whale species, when you come to study them, are actually remarkably different from one another.'

'It's the same with telling individual grey whales apart too,' Marina said. 'Some have missing bits from their fins or their flukes. Others have unique markings on their skin caused by the parasites.'

She clicked a new tab on the laptop, and suddenly onscreen appeared a picture of the entire Pacific coastline. At various points along the coast were blue dots.

'What are those?' Rio asked, leaning forward.

'This is the best bit!' Marina said excitedly. 'Each of those blue dots is actually a grey whale!'

'The whales who are easily identifiable,' Birch said, 'we can track using the GPS coordinates of where they were each sighted along the coastline.'

Marina zoomed in and clicked on one of the dots. 'See this whale?'

The blue dot got larger and larger until it filled the screen completely.

'That's White Beak.'

Chapter Fourteen

A Lucky Idea

Rio was so in shock he couldn't even speak. All he could do was open and close his mouth like a fish.

'That's her at the start of her migration off the coast of Vancouver in Canada,' said Marina. 'Someone must have spotted her and taken a photo. That's how we know it's White Beak.' She pointed to another blue dot. 'This one is her in San Francisco not that long ago.'

The feeling in Rio's belly was as if someone had let off a firecracker and it was fizzing round his insides. Up until a few days ago, White Beak had been just a piece of paper. A drawing that had linked him to his mum while he was thousands of miles away from her.

But now, as Rio gazed at the screen, something shifted in his heart. Because it wasn't just a blue dot. Or a piece of paper. It was a living, breathing whale. A whale who had once meant something very special to his mother.

White Beak had been the first whale his mum had ever seen, and he had witnessed from the photos in the museum just how happy this had made her. Not sad and depressed like she'd been when he'd left her in London. Not *that* version of Mum. The one who spent hours locked in her shell and sometimes did strange things. The other one. The one who smiled as if she had sunshine in her soul.

As he looked at the blue dot again, Rio realised he wasn't just looking at a whale. He was looking at a far better way to save his mother.

Sending photos of different whales was a great idea but this? This was *perfect*. Because surely, if there was anything that could really help her, it would be White Beak. The most beautiful reminder of how happy she'd once been . . . and how happy she could be again.

It didn't make much sense. Not on the surface anyway. The whole notion that sending photos of a specific whale would make a difference. But as soon as the idea was in Rio's head, he couldn't dislodge the image of Mum's smile as she came face to face with White Beak once more. The way her eyes would light up! How she would beam!

There was only one problem. How on earth could he get photos of White Beak? He supposed he could take some off the database. That would . . .

Out of nowhere, Marina started laughing. Not a horrible laugh but a fat, giggly one that was so infectious Rio found himself smiling without even knowing why.

'Rio, you must be the luckiest person I've ever met!'

she said, grinning so broadly he could almost see every tooth in her mouth.

'Me? Lucky?' he replied. 'Why?'

'Don't you see?' she exclaimed, still giggling and pointing to the screen. 'Don't you see where White Beak is?'

Rio shook his head, confused.

'She's here!' said Marina. 'She's about to pass Ocean Bay any day now.'

'*What?*' Rio asked breathlessly.

'Yes!' Marina laughed. 'You might get to see her with your own eyes!'

CHAPTER FIFTEEN

The Boat Trip

'YOU CAN'T COME all this way to Ocean Bay and *not* do a boat trip,' Fran said the next morning over breakfast. 'See? Even Pirate approves.'

The cat, who was perched on Fran's lap, meowed in agreement.

Rio let out the biggest sigh of relief in the entire world.

He had been so afraid his grandmother would find some excuse to say no. Back home, Mum got anxious about him crossing the road to buy a pint of milk, let alone going out on the wild ocean.

But he truly was going to see the grey whales today. And not just any whales – he might even get to spot White Beak! Although Birch had played down the possibility of sighting her, Rio's veins still fizzed and thrummed with excitement.

He hadn't confided in Fran about the possibility of seeing Mum's whale. And he most certainly hadn't told her anything about his plan. After all, he knew what grown-ups were like. They spoiled things with logic. And Rio didn't need logic right now. He just needed hope.

'Anyway,' Fran said, interrupting his thoughts, 'it's about time you did some normal things.'

Rio looked up in surprise. Going to school was normal. Looking after Mum was normal. But going out on the ocean? That was anything but normal!

'Just make sure you wear a life jacket at all times,' she said, grabbing her car keys. 'No getting too close to the edge of the boat and definitely do not lean out over the water or any of the silly things you young people get up to.'

Rio could have remarked that he wasn't about to do anything of the sort, but she had already bundled him out of the door and before he knew it, they were on their way. At the marina they found Birch chatting to a young couple on the jetty.

'Hello!' Fran called out.

'I thought that was you!' Marina appeared on deck, her hair blowing wildly in the breeze. At first, Rio thought she was speaking to him, but then he realised she was actually talking to Fran. 'What? Hang on – Mrs Gilbert is your *grandmother*?'

Fran put a protective hand on his shoulder. 'Hello, Marina. Yes, this is my grandson, Rio.'

'You two know each other?' Rio gasped.

Not just that but from the warmth of their greeting

they also appeared to be *friends*. Of course, Ocean Bay was tiny compared to London, but he never would have guessed in a million years that someone like Marina would be friends with his grandmother.

'Mrs Gilbert used to be my teacher,' Marina explained. 'It was thanks to your grandma that I passed my science exams last year.'

'Now, now,' Fran said gruffly.

Before Rio could question either of them, Marina jumped down on to the jetty and started chattering away to her. He watched them, amazed. Because in Marina's presence it was as if his grandmother was a photograph that had just been filtered with a stronger, brighter colour. Now she was even laughing! Not just polite laughing but proper belly laughing at what Marina said. And in that moment Rio felt the teeniest sliver of guilt because he had never stopped to consider that there might be a different side to his grandmother.

'You made it then,' Birch said, materialising next to them with a warm smile of welcome.

'I trust you'll take good care of him,' Fran said, gripping Rio's shoulders tightly.

'You know full well the *Spyhopper* has the best safety record in Ocean Bay,' Birch stated.

She nodded. 'I wouldn't let him go out with anyone else.'

'Come with us if you'd like?' Rio said impulsively, turning to his grandmother. 'I mean, if there's space?'

Fran looked startled, and, if the sunlight hadn't been so bright, Rio would have sworn she was blushing. 'Thank you, Rio. But . . . but not for me. Not because I don't want to. But boat travel and I have never been the best of friends.'

Rio nodded, unsure if he felt relieved or not.

'Well, be safe.' She smiled awkwardly at him. 'And have a good time.'

Birch ushered Rio and the young couple up on deck where a small huddle of eager tourists awaited them. Today he was wearing a black T-shirt, which on the front had silvery, hand-stitched lettering saying *Spyhopper*

Whale-watching Tours above a picture of a grey whale. As Marina jumped back on deck, Rio noticed that under her red dungarees she wore the same.

Among the tourists were the young couple, who were from Philadelphia, a trainee marine biologist called Fernanda from just over the border in Mexico and a pair of twins who had travelled all the way from Finland. Birch positioned himself at the wheel while everyone sat on the bench seating, chattering excitedly.

Rio was about to take a seat – somewhere safe and secure in the middle of the boat – when Marina hurriedly beckoned him to the bow, the pointy bit at the front.

'It's the best place to be!' she said excitedly, instructing him to lie flat on his tummy with his head poking over the very end of the boat. 'Means we're the first ones to see anything.'

The bow might be the best place to be, but Rio gulped nervously, especially when the boat slid away from her moorings. He wasn't the strongest swimmer – he hated being out of his depth in the local pool. And even though

Marina had reassured him that the *Spyhopper* was perfectly safe, he couldn't help but worry. What if they capsized or sank or got lost out at sea? Luckily, he had left the picture of White Beak at home for safekeeping.

But it was too late for second thoughts now. The *Spyhopper* moved steadily under the tall shadow of the lighthouse, drawing level with the harbour walls before finally coming face to face with the open water. Here the waves became choppier, rising higher, with one or two slapping over the bow. Rio's stomach lurched.

He gripped tighter on to his life jacket and peered downwards, through the surface of the waves, to the invisible depths below. At first, he couldn't see anything except the movement of the water itself. This living, moving thing that pushed and pulled against the hull and sprayed up into his face. The sea salt was making his skin tighten, and his elbows already ached from leaning on the hard wooden hull. It was as if he hadn't just left the harbour but had instead entered an entire new universe.

'Isn't it amazing?' Marina shouted across.

His eyes were already sore and, as the boat dipped, his tummy heaved once again. But, to his complete and utter surprise, Rio agreed. 'Yes,' he whispered.

And because the ocean was wild, and the wind was whipping their words far out to sea, and because he felt the cry rise up from somewhere deep within, he yelled with every ounce of his being.

'YES!'

As the *Spyhopper* left the shore behind, Rio felt something inside loosen. Something he didn't even know had been tied up at all.

Chapter Sixteen

Out on the Ocean

The *Spyhopper* headed out into open water, then turned south with the aim of circling back to harbour in an hour. Even though it was uncomfortable resting on his elbows, and his knees were starting to ache, Rio kept his eyes glued to the water.

It was only a matter of minutes before he saw his

first fish, silver and mercurial, flashing under the surface. Then another – this one bigger, darting through the waves. And there – a splash of water as a fish jumped briefly into the air before zipping quickly back below.

Marina jabbed him in the ribs and pointed out two birds with huge beaks circling in the blue sky. 'Pelicans,' she murmured, fishing in her pockets for her binoculars. 'See how the underside of their beak is all saggy? That's their throat pouch. They use it to scoop up fish. Watch. I think one of them's about to dive.'

Rio pulled out the binoculars Marina had given him and kept his eye on the pelican. A strange-looking, prehistoric creature. He had seen them before in London in St James's Park but not out on the great ocean. Not like *this*. The bird circled in the sky before suddenly diving headfirst into the water and landing with a splash, re-emerging with a fish hanging from its bill.

'The ocean is hard,' Marina said as if sensing his sympathy for the fish. 'It's the hardest, most dangerous place on earth. But in other ways it's also the most *in* danger.'

Rio sneaked a sideways look at her. Although his own stomach was still rolling, Marina seemed completely at home. As though she were a mermaid carved out of the boat itself and had been born to live on the sea. He didn't think he had ever felt that same sense of belonging anywhere.

'Dolphin!' Fernanda yelled excitedly. 'There!!!'

As if conjured up out of a magic box hidden just below the surface of the water, a dolphin emerged, its sleek grey body arching out of the waves before it dived back in.

'Bottlenose!' Marina shouted, standing up. 'See the pointy shape of its snout?'

'There's loads!' Rio cried. Suddenly the water was alive with them, writhing and dancing and jumping in every direction.

'They want to play!' Birch shouted, roaring the engine into life as the boat surged forward.

'Look down!' Marina said.

Just beneath the surface, four dolphins swam alongside the *Spyhopper*, keeping pace with the speed of the boat effortlessly.

Rio screamed with laughter. The faster the boat went, the harder the dolphins raced, leaping joyfully through the water right next to the bow. There were no words. Just this wondrous feeling rushing through his blood like magic.

It was better than any rollercoaster, better even than the time Mum had taken him to the fairground. It was all of that. And yet more. Marina let out a loud scream, pure joy etched on every part of her face. The kind of joy Rio hadn't felt in such a long time. Had maybe never expected to feel again, and yet being out here it zipped and coursed through his veins like electricity.

Just as quickly as the dolphins had appeared, they disappeared, and the boat slowed down to its normal speed before Birch cut the engine altogether. Rio pulled himself upright, rubbing his elbows. Behind them was the coastline, indistinct and blurry. Hardly real at all.

Without the engine noise, the sound of the waves slapping against the hull was much louder. A steady *thwack-thwack* sound.

No one in the boat spoke. But that didn't mean it was silent. Because it was the sound of anticipation. The kind an audience makes before the concert begins. Something trembling and alive.

'We're looking for the grey whales now,' Marina

whispered. 'This is the spot where we usually see them. Just keep your eyes peeled. They could be anywhere.'

This was it. Even though there was no guarantee they would see White Beak, Rio's heart quickened and he had a sudden, fierce desire for his mother to be here with him. An urge so powerful he gripped on to the side of the boat to steady himself. She might not be here. But *he* was. And he would be her eyes.

'How long do we wait?' Rio whispered back, not really sure why they were whispering, but only that out in the ocean he sensed loud voices didn't belong.

'There's no way of telling,' murmured Marina. 'We just have to be patient.'

The couple from Philadelphia had pulled out the largest camera Rio had ever seen and were busy scanning it across the horizon with a series of rapid clicks. The twins and Fernanda were on the other side of the boat, leaning over the edge and peering into the distance with bright, hopeful expressions and wind-coarsened cheeks. And even though Birch must have taken the boat out hundreds, thousands of times before, he too had an expression on his face that was full of wonder.

Rio wondered if that was how *he* looked too. As if being out here had rubbed away some earthly essence of his.

'Why have we stopped?' one of the twins asked.

'We cut the engine because we don't want to frighten the whales,' Birch explained to everyone. 'If we see a whale, then we allow it to come to us – *not* the other way around. The ocean is *their* world. And it's important to always remember that we're just its guests.'

The waves kept on slapping against the hull, and even the boat itself appeared to be waiting.

'We're looking for whale plumes,' Marina said quietly. 'That's the easiest way to spot them. Remember how I said all whales come to the surface to breathe and then take a breath through their blowholes?'

While Marina retrieved her notebook from her pocket to record any grey whales they saw, Rio looked through his binoculars. They were tiny but powerful and brought the far distance into startling clarity. What had looked like white specks with his own eyesight transformed into pelicans resting on the ocean surface. Far out to sea, he could see the outline of a sailing vessel, gulls swarming round it hungrily.

But what he didn't see was a . . .

'WHALE!'

Chapter Seventeen

Heart-shaped Rainbows

'There!' Marina shouted excitedly, jabbing her hand towards the horizon. Rio nearly dropped the binoculars as everyone rushed over, throwing themselves to the edge of the boat and making the *Spyhopper* tilt and roll under their weight.

Marina grabbed Rio's hand and redirected it, so his

gaze would follow. 'See? Five o'clock. A grey whale!'

Rio's eyes widened because there it was. Not even fifty metres away. The most magnificent spurt of water erupting out of the ocean surface like an upside-down waterfall.

The breath of a whale.

From shore, it had been impossible to hear the whale breathing. But out here, with the engine quietened, the loud whooshing sound reverberated off the water and sent tingles down his spine.

But it wasn't even the sound of its breath that was the most miraculous thing.

It was the shape.

The breath didn't just spurt upwards in a vertical line of exhaled water – it was in the shape of a heart.

'How do they do that?' He turned to Marina in astonishment.

'It's because they have two blowholes unlike a lot of other whales who just have one,' Marina explained, bringing her hands together to demonstrate. 'When they breathe, the two plumes of water meet at the top like this, and it looks as if they're breathing out hearts.'

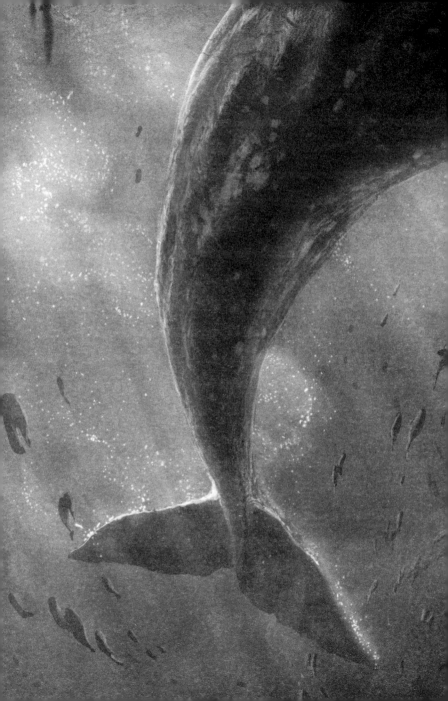

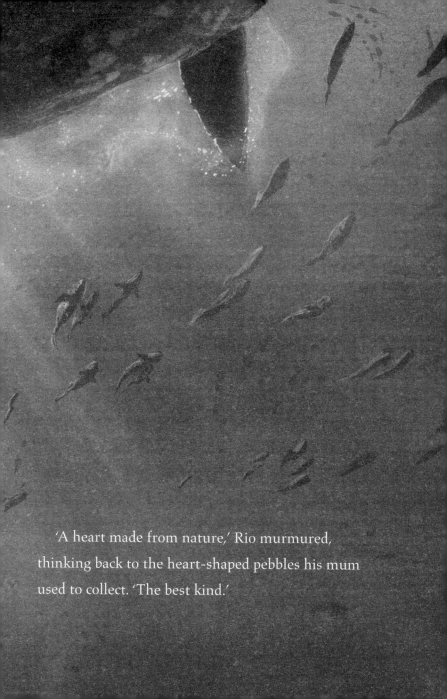

'A heart made from nature,' Rio murmured, thinking back to the heart-shaped pebbles his mum used to collect. 'The best kind.'

He turned back to the water and waited in hushed anticipation for the whale to emerge.

'Any minute now, it'll resurface,' said Marina quietly. 'And this time look extra closely at the heart.'

Rio fixed his gaze on the spot where the whale had been. The light off the water was so bright that it rippled upwards in a shimmery blue haze. And just as his elbows were beginning to throb, and he didn't think he could hold his position a minute longer, he heard it. The sharp whoosh of breath as the whale exhaled once more. This time even closer to the boat – so close someone screamed.

As Rio leaned forward, he couldn't help but let out a gasp. Because illuminated in the whale's heart-shaped breath was the most beautiful sight he had ever seen.

'A *rainbow*?'

'Not just a rainbow,' Marina whispered. 'A rainbow heart.'

Glistening and shining as if the heart were made of magic. The *best* kind of magic.

'It's the oil in their breath catching the sun's rays,' she explained.

Around him the cameras clicked and whirred, but Rio was frozen to the spot. He couldn't describe the feeling that coursed through his body. It was nothing he had ever felt before. Nothing like being at the zoo where there was a wall or a fence between him and the animals. This was complete wildness. Something pure and untouched and free.

His mind flashed back to the photo of Mum on the boat. The joy on her face and the light in her eyes. No wonder! It was at this precise moment that Rio finally understood why she had loved the whales so much. Because who couldn't fail to love an animal that made rainbows?

'It's swimming away,' Marina said. 'Check out the tail.'

Through the binoculars, Rio watched as the huge tail flicked once, then twice before slipping back into the water and disappearing. Only after the whale had gone did Rio wonder if it could have been White Beak. It had been impossible to tell. In fact, everything had happened so quickly, he'd not even taken any photos.

Just as he was cursing himself for being so slow, Rio heard something.

Not the *thwack-thwack* of the waves, or the *click-click* of the cameras, or even the cry of the gulls or the excited chatter of the humans. Something else entirely. An echo rising up from the depths. A strange rumbling, groaning noise he had never heard before.

'That noise . . .'

'What noise?' Marina said, turning to him. 'The water slapping against the hull?'

'No. Not that. The *other* noise.'

'The other noise?' Marina looked puzzled. 'You mean the engine?'

Rio shook his head and tried to listen. But whatever it was had gone. Disappeared into the depths. He settled himself back down and lay with his fingers trailing above the water. As Marina filled in her notebook, he felt a sense of relaxation drift over him. How strange that he didn't feel self-conscious or shy or anxious, or any of the things he tended to experience on land. He felt – and this sounded a bit silly even to his own ears as it was only his first-ever boat ride – almost at *home*.

Even if he didn't get to see White Beak today, just knowing she was close by gave Rio a curious sense of comfort. As if his mother was here with him. That he could almost hear her voice whispering to him across the ocean.

The sound was so vivid that he sat up. He wasn't imagining things. He *could* hear something. The same echoey noise he'd heard just moments earlier. Rio looked around. Marina was still making notes about the whale they'd just seen, while Birch was describing migratory behaviour to the others.

It was only Rio who saw it.

Hiding under the surface of the water about three metres away from the bow end.

Rio felt his whole body still, the way Mum did before

playing the first note on her violin, as if she were tuning herself with the instrument in some magical, unseen way. As if there were an invisible current linking him to the whale and, by keeping himself motionless, he could somehow reach out and connect with it.

All of a sudden, the whale pushed its head out of the ocean, and it was so close, and so sudden, that Marina dropped her notebook. 'Oh my!'

The others in the boat rushed over to the bow and, over his shoulder, Rio heard the *click-click* of the camera and the gasps of those behind him. But none of that registered because the whale right in front of his eyes looked remarkably familiar.

'White Beak!'

Chapter Eighteen

White Beak

IN REAL LIFE, the whale was so big, so vast, so awe-inspiring that Rio bit his tongue – the hot, metallic taste of blood filling his mouth. Her head alone was probably three times the size of Rio, made up of one huge upper and lower jaw. The skin was a dark slate colour with patches of lighter grey and white covering her nose.

'It's her!' Marina yelled triumphantly. 'It's White Beak!'

Rio couldn't even answer. Instead, he just gazed at the whale with pure, unblinking longing. Because surely this wasn't just a coincidence? It was a *sign*. A sign, as clear as day, that he was on the right track to helping Mum and making her better again. Otherwise, why would White Beak appear at this exact moment?

The whale's head was probably out of the water mere seconds, but it was as if time had stopped, and in that way Rio managed to drink in every last detail. The crinkly outline round her one visible eye, how the barnacles stuck to her snout in coarse, uneven clumps, the white meshy stuff in her mouth that Marina had said was called baleen.

But then, just as quickly as she had appeared, the whale was gone.

'Did you see?!' Marina was jumping up and down for joy. 'Did you see the way she was looking at you?'

Rio nodded, although his gaze was still fixed on the

water, praying for White Beak to resurface so he could take photos. Just wait until Mum saw this! Just wait till she discovered that Rio had found her whale. He hurriedly fished in his pocket for his phone.

The others were crowding round his back, standing so close he could smell them. It made retrieving his phone more awkward, but if he shuffled forward a bit . . .

. . . and then he wasn't quite sure what happened next.

Except that he lost his footing and since there was nothing to hold on to at the bow, Rio stood for a moment, suspended in thin air, with his arms flailing like a windmill.

The next thing he knew he entered the water with a very loud and very cold splash.

Even though he was wearing a life jacket, Rio's entire body, including his head, dropped below the surface. It was so sudden and so frightening that the first thing he did was open his mouth to shout for help. Which was a silly thing to do because the seawater rushed in and then he was spitting and gagging and coughing. By the time he had bobbed back up to the surface, the boat looked frighteningly far away. All he could see was the slippery grey hull and seven very pale faces peering over the edge.

'RIO!' Marina yelled. 'Stay there and don't panic!'

Don't panic? It was too late for that. Rio flailed his arms and thrashed his legs desperately. He couldn't even *see* the bottom, let alone touch it. There was just a vast well of horribly dark water and the sensation of knowing he was way, way out of his depth.

'MARINA!' he shouted, just as another wave splattered against him. He gasped in shock. '*MARINA!*'

Birch leaned over the boat, holding out a long pole with a hook on the end. 'Stay calm, Rio. Grab hold of this and I'll pull you in.'

Rio stretched out an arm and tried to grasp the hook. He nearly had it when a wave shoved him roughly aside. He coughed and spluttered and gagged. Then he tried again. But, as much as he desperately tried to reach the pole, the current kept pushing him backwards.

It was then Rio remembered he wasn't alone.

There was also a sixteen-metre-long grey whale in the water with him.

Marina had said grey whales weren't dangerous. That they would never deliberately hurt a human. But it was easy to think that if you were looking at them from the safe, dry deck of a boat. Not when you were actually *in* the water with them and they had a mouth bigger than your entire body.

Just as he was about to enter full panic mode, Rio heard the same echoey noise as before, except this time it was much closer. He cocked an ear. He definitely was *not* imagining it. The noise sounded deep and shadowy and bass-like. A series of low rumbles followed by a click, then a drumming and another click. The only way to describe it was like a ripple coming up from somewhere beneath the surface of the water and travelling up through the soles of his feet.

But *where* was it coming from?

It was a strange and unworldly sound but not, Rio

realised gratefully, a threatening one. Instead, it was almost comforting – like one of those bedtime stories his mother used to tell of faraway, mystical lands and strange, mythical creatures that used to lull him to sleep.

And Rio knew in his heart that it was White Beak.

As if in agreement, he felt a gentle nudge on his back.

His first reaction was to spin round. But turning round in water wasn't easy. All Rio ended up doing was flopping face down. He gasped for air, swallowed some more seawater before finally managing to manoeuvre himself the right way up.

She was so close, he could see the individual barnacles lining the right side of her face, how the white pigmentation covered nearly all of her upper jaw, but was patchier round the very tip of the snout. And he could smell her skin – brine and oil and fish. He should have been scared. But somehow he wasn't.

'Hello, White Beak,' he whispered. 'It *is* you, isn't it?'

Rio wanted to reach out and touch her, but he didn't dare. There was something precious about the whale that

commanded respect, like Mum's most expensive violin – the one she only used for important concerts – which she kept wrapped up in its case at all times when not in use.

'You're beautiful,' he murmured, his voice cracking.

From nowhere, a burst of emotion filled his chest, so hard and so bright he had to close his eyes momentarily. When he opened them again, White Beak was right in front of him, gazing at Rio in a way that made his heart tremble. It didn't make any sense. Not logically anyway. But it was the same way Mum used to gaze at him.

Full of love.

The thought that such love could come from a wild animal should have felt strange. Especially from an animal who had been so mistreated by humans. But somehow it didn't. In fact, it felt as though this love had always been there and always would be. Theirs was a bond as old as time and as deep as the ocean.

From behind him, Rio could hear the calls from those on the boat getting increasingly louder and more shrill.

By now, his legs were tired from treading water and his eyes stung so much he could barely even see. But, despite all this, he didn't want to turn round. Not yet.

'I . . . I . . .' He wanted to say something but he wasn't sure what. What could you say to such a creature? The whale looked at him one last time and then began to slowly lower her head.

Rio's whole body was beginning to ache now from being in the water. White Beak dipped her nose forward and pressed it lightly against his chest. Then she gave him the gentlest of nudges and pushed him back towards the boat. All the while, he kept his eyes pinned to her face as she slowly slipped under the water and disappeared beneath the surface.

Even though he was now right next to the hull of the *Spyhopper*, and Marina was leaning over the edge, yelling at him to grab the pole, Rio didn't move. Instead, he just stared at the ripples in the water, the only sign that White Beak had been there at all, and wondered why he suddenly felt so alone.

Then, abruptly, he was yanked out of the ocean and hauled over the side of the boat. Once on deck, he coughed and spat out a mouthful of seawater. His eyes stung and his skin felt puckered and cold.

'When I invited you to come whale watching,' Marina said, crouching down next to Rio, 'I didn't mean for you to actually get *in* the water.'

CHAPTER NINETEEN

Smiling

'Do you know,' Fran remarked after a late dinner that same night, 'it's the first time I've actually seen you smile.'

Rio touched the corners of his lips with his fingers. He hadn't even realised he had been smiling. But yes. His lips were turned upwards. It was so unfamiliar that he dropped his hands in shock.

'The grey whale,' she said, 'is quite simply one of the most magnificent animals on earth. And, like all wild animals, they have the power to transcend almost anything.'

Unable to contain his excitement, Rio had told her about coming face to face with a grey whale. Although he had chosen to leave out the fact it was White Beak and that he'd fallen into the water. Those parts he kept to himself.

'I remember the first time I ever saw one,' murmured Fran. 'Oh, a long time ago now, but the feeling never leaves you.'

Her face took on a distant, faraway expression. A look that was remarkably similar to the ones he'd seen on the faces of the whale watchers. So much so that Rio was almost tempted to tell her about his plan to save Mum. Because perhaps she could help?

He was debating whether or not he could trust her when the phone rang.

Of course, it was Sunday! His whole body was still tingling so much after meeting White Beak that it took him a moment to realise this was the call he'd been waiting for all week. Mum had switched the time to the evening, which meant it must be really early in the morning over there.

As before, Fran answered and then passed the phone over.

'Mum?' Rio scampered out to the back step where the sun was low in the sky. 'Guess who I saw today?' he said, too excited to hold it in for a second longer. 'You won't guess, but it was White Beak! Your whale! I saw her in the ocean with my own eyes!'

He paused to catch his breath. His heart was pitter-pattering like rain against his chest. Waiting for her to react. Waiting for her to say something.

'*Mum?*'

'I'm here,' she said in a voice that sounded so far away Rio had to press the phone harder to his ear. 'You've been on the water?'

Rio swallowed down a sigh. He'd forgotten how he sometimes had to repeat things. *Never mind*. He would speak slower this time, and tell her the whole story from the beginning.

'I met a girl on the pier. Marina. And then she took me whale watching on her boat and . . .'

'You went to the marina?'

'I did . . . but *first* I went to the pier. The girl I met – *she's* called Marina.'

'Marina,' said his mum. 'What a lovely name.'

The sun was slipping fast in the sky, now so low it was touching the surface of the water. Rio hurried on. 'Didn't you hear me, Mum? I saw White Beak! I saw your whale!'

'My whale?' For the first time, her tone brightened. 'White Beak? You mean *my* White Beak?'

'That's right. Your White Beak,' Rio said, just as the sun sank below the horizon in a dazzling flash of gold. 'I saw her today.'

There was a long silence. So long he thought his

heart would burst. But eventually he heard the tiniest of sounds. The sound of his mother's smile.

CHAPTER TWENTY

Photos Home

BEFORE GOING TO sleep, Rio lay face down on the bed with his grandmother's laptop. He had asked to borrow it the other day so he could do some of his school homework. Which wasn't altogether a lie as his school was sending him assignments. But this was studying of a different kind. It was the study of White Beak. His

own phone now lay at the bottom of the Pacific Ocean.
But luckily the couple from Philadelphia had said they
were going to email him some of the photos they took.

Rio was so impatient his fingers clicked and clacked
the wrong key before finally he managed to get into his
inbox.

Please *be there*.

And yes! There they were!

He gasped. They were the most magnificent photos
he had ever seen. Far better than anything he could have
taken on his own phone. So vivid and alive it was as if
he was in the water again and face to face with a wild
grey whale.

Not just *any* whale either. White Beak.

She was lying next to the boat, so close to the surface
you could almost see the outline of her entire body, and
it filled the picture completely. The sheer size of her was
breathtaking. She was the most gigantic creature he had
ever seen. Far bigger than the *Spyhopper* and yet, as Rio
zoomed in on her face, there was a gentleness about her

too. A gentleness that didn't come from size – but from the inside.

'You're not just an animal, are you?' he whispered, touching the screen. 'You're like us.'

He felt a bit silly saying that because whales weren't humans. But still. There was something special about White Beak. Not just how she had gazed at him in that peculiarly human way, but also the way she had nudged him safely back to the boat as if she were taking care of him. As if somehow she were looking out for him. Without even knowing why, Rio felt his throat thicken. He'd been in Ocean Bay just over a week. And, up until today, it had been the loneliest week of his life.

However, suddenly Rio didn't feel quite so alone.

'I found you,' he said softly. 'Or maybe you found me.'

He went to stand by the window, positioning himself in his mum's footprints, and contemplated the water. The only sad thing was that he wouldn't see her again. Marina had explained that White Beak, like all the grey whales, was just passing by Ocean Bay on her way south to the lagoons. It had been mere chance he had seen her at all. But even though the encounter had been brief, perhaps lasting only minutes, Rio knew he would remember it for the rest of his life.

'You helped me,' he murmured. 'And now you're going to help Mum too.'

The next call with his mother wouldn't be for two weeks as next Sunday she'd be in a special class or something. Two weeks. It would be a *long* wait. But, by then, she should be feeling much better.

Especially after he'd sent her these photos of White Beak. What better way of reminding Mum of how happy she'd been as a child and more importantly, how happy she could be again?

Rio hadn't mentioned he was going to send pictures as sometimes she got a bit confused when he told her too many things at once. This would be an extra-special surprise.

It took several attempts to find the right words to

accompany the email. But, in the end, he decided on something short and simple.

Dear Mum,

Here are some photos of White Beak. She was passing by Ocean Bay today and I saw her with my own eyes. Other than you, she was the most incredible thing I've ever seen and made my insides happy.

I hope she makes you happy too.

Love

Rio-cat xxx

Rio sent the email with a grin and then crossed another day off his calendar. Only three weeks to go until Mum got better and he could go home.

Chapter Twenty-one

Special Hearing

'Are you ready?' asked Marina, wearing the kind of grin that comes from the taste of adventure on your lips combined with the added bonus of finishing school for the day. It was the afternoon whale-watching trip and she had insisted Rio join her and Birch on the ocean. And he wasn't about to say no to that. Apart from the three of them, there was a sizeable group of Japanese tourists, a teacher from Washington and a middle-aged couple from Scotland.

Like the day before, Birch directed the *Spyhopper* southbound to an area well away from the busy entrance to the marina. Today the water was choppier, the waves smacking the hull, with the occasional white horse flecking the surface.

Even though Rio's stomach lurched up and down, he didn't feel seasick. In fact, it was hard to imagine he had ever been afraid of the sea. Everything was so much bigger and brighter out there. As if the sun had been turned up a notch and had left a dusting of gold all over the surface of the world.

After ten minutes or so, they reached their destination and Birch cut the engine. It didn't matter that the boat was full of a completely different set of tourists. The same hushed anticipation filled the air. Hope so sharp that Rio could taste it.

But, unlike yesterday, there was one thing missing.

Whales.

For half an hour, the boat bobbed up and down silently with not a whale in sight. Not a tail. Not a spyhop. Not a plume. And most definitely no heart-shaped rainbows.

'That's the thing,' Marina remarked as some of the tourists grew impatient. 'The whales don't work on human time.'

Rio wanted to agree. He really did. But it was difficult not to quell the rising sense of disappointment in his belly. He'd desperately wanted to see more whales. Not just for his mother, but also, he realised, for *him* too. Meeting Marina and being onboard the *Spyhopper* had given him the most joy he'd had for the longest of times. A chance to live a life he never could have imagined for himself. But how many more boat trips would Marina realistically invite him on while he was in Ocean Bay? Birch had said how busy they were going to be in the next few weeks. What if this trip was Rio's very last chance to see the whales?

It was then he heard a click. So soft that at first he

thought he'd mistaken it. But there! Another click. Rio listened hard. It was the same noise as yesterday. A long, garbled gurgle, then a series of short, sharp clicks followed by a noise that sounded like a bass drum.

He spun round, scanning the water from all angles. But, however hard he looked, there was nothing to see. Yet he could still hear something. He was *sure* he could. Where was it coming from?

Over there. It was coming from beneath the water over there.

'There's a whale!' he said hurriedly as Birch got ready to start the engine. 'Five o'clock.'

Marina squinted hard in the direction Rio was pointing. 'I can't see anything.'

'There is one. I can hear it,' he said urgently. '*Over there!*'

At which point, a ginormous, barnacled head burst out of the water at the exact point where Rio had been pointing.

'A spyhop!' someone yelled.

The whale gazed around before sinking majestically back beneath the waves. As the occupants of the boat sprang to life, taking photos and chattering animatedly, Marina looked curiously at Rio as if he was a puzzle she was trying to work out.

'How did you know the whale was there?'

'I heard it,' he said. 'Didn't you?'

She frowned. 'But you *can't* hear them!'

'Why not?'

'Because humans can't hear grey whales,' Marina answered. 'Their pitch is too low for our ears. It would be like you hearing a dog whistle. It's just not possible.'

Rio pictured the moment when he had been in the water and heard the sounds travelling up through his feet. It had definitely come from White Beak. Just as the noise he had heard moments ago had definitely come from that whale. He knew it in the same way he could sense when a storm was coming because of the crackle of electricity in the air. Mum said it was because he had cat's ears. 'But I did hear it. I swear I did!'

Marina wrinkled her brow before sweeping her hand out. 'You swear on the ocean? You *swear* you can hear them?'

He nodded. 'Ocean's promise!'

'Okay, what about now then?' she said. 'Can you hear one now?'

Rio closed his eyes. He concentrated hard, trying to block out the sound of the water thwacking against the hull, the conversation of the other passengers, even the intensity of Marina's gaze, which he could feel on his face.

At first, he heard nothing, and a tiny seed of doubt crept in. Maybe he'd been wrong? But then a tiny click. Faint but definitely there. A gurgle. Another click. Now he just had to figure out the direction.

'Eleven o'clock,' he said decisively.

Marina swung herself round and stared at the horizon with such ferocious intensity that Rio shivered. The ocean remained calm and flat.

He gulped. *Come on.* He couldn't be wrong.

Still nothing.

And then . . . a plume of water shooting high in the sky.

Marina spun back round, regarding Rio with a mixture of awe and wonder. 'You really can hear them!'

Chapter Twenty-two

Invitation

THE REST OF that boat trip, Marina and Rio had fun experimenting. What was the sound really like? Could he try and describe it to her? How far away did the whale need to be in order for him to hear it? Marina even made diagrams in her notebook to show the approximate distances.

'This is us on the boat,' she explained. 'And the furthest whale was over here, which is about one hundred metres, I would guess.'

'I only heard that one really faintly.'

'But it's still incredible!' Marina turned to Rio with eyes that shone like stars. 'I've been on the water since I was a baby and I've *never* heard the grey whales. But you can!'

Rio shook his head in disbelief. How strange to think he'd come all this way to the other side of the world to discover something so unusual about himself. He had only just begun to start processing it when the *Spyhopper* docked back at the jetty and Marina ran up to Birch and grabbed his arm.

'Dad! You'll never guess! Rio can hear the grey whales!'

Rio thought Birch was going to instantly dismiss it. The kind of reaction grown-ups gave a lot when they heard something that seemed far-fetched. But he did nothing of the sort. Instead, he narrowed his eyes and chewed his lip thoughtfully.

'I could tell there was something different about you the first time we went out on the water.' He paused. 'You've got the ocean's ear, as we sailors would say.'

Marina glanced up at her dad and something passed between them. Rio wasn't quite sure exactly what, but it was as if there were invisible words floating in the air and a conversation taking place out of sight.

Birch cleared his throat. 'I have only ever heard of one other person in my lifetime who was able to hear the grey whales and that was a Mexican friend of mine from years and years ago who lived down in the lagoons.'

'It must be because of the orchestra,' said Rio. 'That's where I grew up. My mum . . . my mum was a violinist – *is* a violinist. M-m-maybe that's why. I just hear things differently.'

That was the most *logical* explanation – the fact that he'd grown up around musicians – but something else nudged against his ribcage. Something that didn't really make sense. Because he had the strangest sensation that he'd been born for this. Just as Mum had been born for the orchestra or Marina had been born for the ocean. Apparently, and for a reason he couldn't yet understand, Rio had been born to hear grey whales.

Wordlessly, Birch disappeared back into the cabin before returning to the deck. He held out a familiar black T-shirt. On the front was a picture of a grey whale and the silvery, hand-stitched lettering of *Spyhopper Whale-watching Tours*.

'Welcome to the *Spyhopper* crew,' Birch said, offering Rio the T-shirt. 'That is, if you would like to join us? We could do with an extra pair of eyes *and* ears to help us.'

'But . . . I'm only here for another three weeks and then I'm going home.'

'It doesn't matter,' Birch replied. 'Someone with your talent will be priceless in helping us count the whales.'

'Please say yes, Rio!' said Marina. 'With your help, just think how many more whales we can save!'

'Save? What do you mean?' Rio asked. 'Humans don't hunt them as much any more, do they?'

'They don't,' said Birch. 'But unfortunately we're still hurting them in numerous other ways.'

'So much plastic ends up in the bellies of whales and dolphins.' Marina shook her head angrily. 'Most of the time, they think it's food.'

'It's not just the plastic,' Birch added. 'The data collected from the Happywhale website helps scientists monitor how rising temperatures are also affecting not just the grey whales' eating habits and behaviour, but all whales out there.'

Plastic pollution along with climate change was something Rio had studied at school. But sitting in a chilly London classroom, looking at photos on the internet, was a long way from being on a boat in the actual Pacific Ocean.

He gulped. 'What do the rising temperatures mean for them?'

Marina took a long, steady look at him before answering. 'It means they're dying.'

'*Dying?*'

'And it's okay for us humans because we can just get out of the water anytime we want.' Marina jabbed her arm in the air. 'But the whales can't. Neither can the turtles, the seals, the walruses, the sea lions or the dolphins. They're *stuck* with it.'

Birch rested a gentle hand on her shoulder. 'My daughter, as you can see, is very passionate on this subject. And rightly so.'

'That's why I studied so hard for my science exams,' she said proudly. 'Because I want to be a marine biologist when I'm older. I want to help save the ocean! But, until then, I'm doing what I can. By counting one whale at a time.'

'The more data we collect,' said Birch, 'the more we help raise awareness of what's happening in the ocean. And awareness is the heart of change.'

He held out the T-shirt. 'None of us can save the world single-handedly. But together we might just stand a chance. Someone like you can truly help us, Rio.'

Marina and Birch were looking at him with such

earnest, hopeful expressions that his own heart leaped in response. Because it wasn't just his mum that needed him any more. It was the entire ocean. And as Rio pulled the T-shirt over the top of his yellow one, he wasn't just slipping on a T-shirt: he was slipping on a whole new identity.

CHAPTER TWENTY-THREE

Training

OVER THE NEXT few days, Birch and Marina taught Rio everything there was to know about becoming a whale-watching guide. Not just the practical aspects – like how the safety of humans and whales always came first – but also the finer details of recording their sightings on the Happywhale database.

By spending time on the *Spyhopper*, Rio learned more about the ocean than he ever could from a book. Whenever he had thought of it previously, it had always been in terms of the crudest statistics and figures. Which ocean was the biggest or the deepest or the coldest. But it wasn't just a *graph*. It was home to millions of animals, some of which most people would never ever see, but that didn't mean they weren't there. It didn't mean they weren't important.

And, since Marina was basically a human encyclopedia when it came to not just grey whales but seemingly every species of marine animal out there, he also hoovered up as much information as he could about the creatures of the deep. It was like being at ocean school.

Rio also learned some sad things too, things that made him feel slightly sick.

How, once upon a time, there were also grey whales in the Atlantic Ocean, but they had been driven to extinction by hunting. That the lagoons of Mexico hadn't always been the safe sanctuaries they are today. Indeed, not even that long ago, the whalers would close off the mouth of a lagoon, trapping all the mothers and calves in there, and then they would slaughter each and every one of them – leaving behind a sea of thick red blood.

But Rio didn't like to dwell on that too much.

In the space of a few minutes with White Beak, he had felt a bond so deep he still heard the faintest echo of it in his heart. The thought of anyone or anything hurting her made his insides shrivel up. Having been face to face with White Beak, he would do everything he could to look after her. At night, tired, sunburnt and dazzled from his day at sea, he had got into the habit of pulling out Mum's picture.

'I'll look after you,' he promised. 'I'll keep you safe.'

He didn't really have any idea *how* he would be able to do that. But at least he could track her on the Happywhale database. While many of the whale sightings came from specialised boat trips, a great deal also came from normal everyday people watching from onshore armed with nothing other than a pair of binoculars and a big dose of patience. Birch even said there was a name for them. They were called citizen scientists.

Rio felt proud to be joining something bigger than himself. But it wasn't just that. Being out in nature and watching the whales gave *him* something back too. Not just the feeling of calm or the taste of adventure but the sense of wonder that only the ocean could provide.

For the longest of times, Rio had been worried. About

his mum primarily. It was hard not to be anxious about her. But also about himself and where someone like him fitted into a world that was often huge and frightening.

But, onboard the *Spyhopper*, Rio finally had a sense of where he belonged and, more importantly, what he could do to help.

CHAPTER TWENTY-FOUR

Happy Times

THE NEXT FEW days were some of the happiest of Rio's life. Days he wished he could bottle and put somewhere safe, so he could open it in the future and relive all the memories again and again and again.

There were two boat trips a day. Each one full of tourists desperate to catch a glimpse of a whale. But for

Rio it wasn't just a trip. It was a chance to realise who he had become. He was only a boy, and yet somehow he was communicating with one of the biggest animals on the planet. It was nothing short of mind-blowing. Each time he heard one, it made his skin go all tingly.

Granted, the whale had to be fairly close by, but Birch insisted that, thanks to Rio, they had vastly increased the number of sightings they made.

'You're making a difference, son,' he said to him one afternoon.

Rio wasn't sure when the older man had started calling him son, but now it had stuck. And, to be honest, he wasn't about to protest. His own dad had never said he was proud of him. But Birch told him every single boat trip.

In return, Rio felt himself stand a little taller.

When she wasn't at school, Marina showed Rio round Ocean Bay. Not just the main boulevards bustling with tourists, but the places only a person who lived there could know about. The garden wall where someone had painted a huge mural of a turtle. The tallest palm tree in town where, once upon a time, Marina had carved her initials with her dad's penknife. The tiny hole at the far end of the pier where, if you pressed your eye against it, you could see shoals of fish swimming beneath you. And the secret ice-cream parlour, tucked away from the main drag, which sold home-made ice cream in a thousand different flavours.

She chattered non-stop. Which was fine by Rio as he had always been more of a listener, and, unlike him, Marina never seemed to run out of words. She told him how she'd learned to swim before she could even walk, that she felt more comfortable with marine animals than she did with humans, and that the first word she'd ever spoken was 'whale'. Her life might have been completely different from his own, but it was also straightforward. As was her relationship with her dad. Just being in their company, Rio felt the jagged edges of his own soul start to soften.

Once in a while, he would be sitting on the *Spyhopper*

and catch a glimpse of his reflection in the water. In just a few weeks, he seemed to have grown sturdier, his face had the same golden glow as Marina's and there was a self-assurance about him that had been missing from his old self back in London.

But despite all this, when he went to bed at night, he still marked off the days on his calendar. Because no matter how many whales he'd heard, or how good a day they'd had on the ocean, the ache in his chest never completely went away. How could it? Not when his mother was in hospital. Not when they'd been separated for the longest-ever time in his life. And missing someone, as Rio found out, was one of the hardest things of all.

He still had to wait three days until he could speak to her, so the next best thing was to stand in her footprints. Just to see if he could somehow magic her up through the floorboards. Besides, he had news to tell her.

'Guess what, Mum? White Beak's been spotted!' he whispered. 'Someone has uploaded a new photo to the database.'

Earlier that day, Marina had excitedly shown him a photo of White Beak swimming past Los Angeles, on her way safely to the lagoons in Mexico. It was an old photo as someone had taken a few days to upload it, but it was still one of the most beautiful pictures Rio had ever seen.

'See, Mum?' he murmured. 'She's going to be all right. Just like you're going to be all right soon too.'

Rio allowed himself a smile. It didn't matter that Mum hadn't replied to any of his emails yet. He was due to talk to her in three days. And then he would tell her *everything*.

Chapter Twenty-five

Fran

I T WAS TOO windy for a boat trip, so Rio was at home with his grandmother. His mind was whirring and spinning with what Mum would say about all the pictures he'd been sending her. The joy in her voice. The sound of her laugh as she explained how seeing White Beak again had reignited something in her heart. How it had—

'Rio?' Fran interrupted his thoughts. 'Are you listening?'

The image of his mother faded, and instead he saw his grandmother's face peering at him over her glasses. It was as if he was climbing up from the bottom of the seabed and surfacing for the first time in weeks. He blinked groggily.

'I said, why don't you tell me more about your whale-watching trips?'

Ever since the first one, Fran had been enthusiastic about Rio's ocean adventures. Each time he'd come home, she'd met him with a hot meal and a dozen curious questions. But whale watching was tiring. And whale listening was even harder. It drained nearly every ounce of his energy. Marina said it was the ocean – it had a way of enveloping almost everything else. All of which meant, when faced with his grandmother's enquiries, he'd usually just yawned before disappearing up to bed to email Mum.

With Pirate perched on her lap, Fran was looking at him in an open, hopeful way. A way that reminded him of the tourists on the *Spyhopper* as they were about to set off on a trip.

Something shameful ran through him. She'd been looking after him, feeding him, washing his clothes, even buying him a new phone to replace the one he'd dropped in the ocean. And what had he given back?

He'd told her almost nothing, save from being invited to become a crew member. Birch always said that the ocean was a two-way thing. If we expected it to look after us – to feed us, to nurture us, to keep us safe – then, in turn, we must look after it.

Rio opened his phone and fished through various pictures before finding the one he wanted. Then he gently slid the phone across the table.

His grandmother picked it up, and then she dropped it again so that it clattered on to the table. 'Is that . . . *White Beak*?'

Rio nodded. He hadn't even been sure whether Fran would know about White Beak, let alone recognise her. Something in his heart softened as she took off her glasses and wiped her eyes.

She picked up the phone again. 'How do I zoom in?'

Rio climbed to her side of the table and showed her. 'See, those are the parasite scars on her snout that we use to identify her.'

'It really is her.' Fran's voice trembled. 'Oh, how your mother loved that whale. How happy it made her.'

Not just happy, but better too, Rio thought.

He pulled up a seat and showed her the rest of the pictures on his phone. Not only the ones of White Beak but also of all the whales he had spotted since arriving in California. For a long time, grandson and grandmother sat shoulder to shoulder at the table, flicking through the footage.

'Just think, by the time you're back in London, White Beak will be in one of the lagoons,' Fran remarked. 'Hopefully, if we're lucky, she'll have a calf too.'

Rio sat up in his chair with a start as his grandmother's words hit home. *He'd be home in just over one week!*

How had the time zipped and sped along so fast? He'd been looking forward to going home for so long, and yet

now it was almost here he didn't know what to think.
Of course, he was buzzing. But as he gazed back down at
the photo of White Beak, something else pressed against
his insides. Something spiky and hard and painful.

'Hopefully, if White Beak does have a calf,' Fran continued, 'that means they'll be spotted passing by Ocean Bay on their way back north. Your mother used to love seeing the calves.'

'Why did she leave?' Rio asked suddenly.

'None of the whales stay in the lagoons that long—'

'No!' he said sharply. '*Mum*. Why did Mum leave Ocean Bay if she loved it here so much?'

Fran seemed startled. She rubbed Pirate's ears before answering.

'Because your mother won the music scholarship,' she said at last. 'It was the hardest decision of her life. To leave and follow her music, or to stay here. In the end, the music won.'

'But what if she had stayed?' Rio asked in a small voice. 'What if she'd stayed in her happy place?'

Fran took a sharp intake of breath. 'Would things have been different, you mean?'

Rio looked down at the table a long time before nodding. He listened to Fran stroking Pirate's head in steady, rhythmical movements until he dared look up.

The expression on his grandmother's face was one he hadn't seen before. But, nevertheless, it was a look he recognised all too well. Because it was a look he had seen every day in the mirror for the past few months. Something raw and naked and fearful.

She had taken off her glasses and was rubbing her eyes wearily.

'To be honest, Rio, no one can know what might have happened if she'd stayed,' Fran said quietly. 'But one thing's for sure: fighting with her because she chose not to come back, well, that was the biggest mistake of all.'

Chapter Twenty-six

Bad News

O<small>N</small> S<small>UNDAY</small> <small>NIGHT</small>, waiting for the phone to ring, Rio's stomach was aflutter with all kinds of nerves. Mum still hadn't replied to his emails but that didn't matter. He would talk to her about the whales. He would speak slowly and clearly and tell her every single thing that had happened in the past few weeks – starting with his ability to hear them and his invitation to join the *Spyhopper* crew.

For the first time since arriving in Ocean Bay, he didn't feel quite so far away from her. He even hummed a little tune to himself under his breath.

The phone burst into life and his heart leaped. He heard Fran answer it. And then . . . and then . . .

What was taking so long?

Instead of passing the phone over, Fran was huddled in the far corner of the kitchen and was gripping it tightly to her ear.

'What? Oh, I see. Well . . .' She lowered her voice. 'How long?'

This was a voice he had not heard his grandmother use before. It was the voice a person might use when expecting bad news. It made Rio's tummy flutter and his throat tighten.

'Right.' She glanced fleetingly at Rio before stepping out into the hallway and gently shutting the kitchen door. Through the glass, he could see her outline – so different from his mother's petite frame – but one, nevertheless, he had got used to. He moved closer to the door, but no matter how hard he listened he couldn't make anything out apart from the low rumble of her voice.

Eventually, Fran came back in and sat down at the table. She twisted her wedding ring round and round her finger before finally looking up. 'That was the doctor . . .' She stopped as if trying to choose the right words. 'Unfortunately, your mother won't be calling you today.'

'Not calling me today?' Rio swallowed. 'You mean she's going to call tomorrow instead? I can speak to her then?'

Fran shook her head. 'The thing is . . . the doctor treating your mom at the clinic says she's taken a very small turn for the worse . . . and that there's a possibility she might have to stay a few weeks longer.'

Weeks? Longer? Rio stared helplessly at his grandmother. *Mum was staying there? She was* worse?

'B-b-but she's supposed to be getting better!' he cried. 'The pictures! I sent her the pictures!'

'What pictures?' Fran asked.

'Pictures of White Beak!' he said angrily, knowing he was shouting but unable to stop himself. 'I've been sending her pictures every night of White Beak and the whales!'

'You have?' Fran looked puzzled. 'But why?'

Rio's heart clawed and ripped and shredded. He wanted to beat his fists against the table. Against himself. Against the world. 'Because the whales made her happy!' he said desperately. 'You said so yourself! You said they were the most magical thing she'd ever seen. That they made her heart smile! And I thought . . .'

'Oh, Rio,' she said softly. 'Oh, my dear child.'

'And now I have to stay here!' he yelled, unable to bear the pity on her face. 'I have to stay here while she's over there, and I can't . . . I can't do anything to help her!'

His grandmother bent over and gripped his shoulders. She leaned forward so close he could smell the peppermint on her breath. 'Rio, listen to me. Nothing you can ever do will make your mother well again. Do you hear me? And that's not because you don't love her. I *know* you love her.' She paused. 'But it's never, *ever* been your responsibility to make her better.'

'But you would say that!' he roared, shrugging her off and unable to stop the words hurling themselves out. 'You're on the other side of the world! You've never been there for her like I have!'

His grandmother opened her mouth to reply but nothing came out. Instead, two growing spots of colour appeared on her cheeks. But still Rio couldn't stop.

'You don't even know what it's like!' he cried. 'I'm the one who's been with her all this time. I'm the one who makes her cups of tea in the middle of the night when she can't sleep. I'm the one who buys her ginger biscuits because she won't eat anything else! I'm the one who holds her hand when she cries. Not you!'

he yelled. 'It's never, *ever* been you!'

His grandmother uttered a small cry. The kind a wounded animal might make. And then Rio ran all the way up the stairs to his room, slammed the door behind him and threw himself on the bed.

CHAPTER TWENTY-SEVEN

Missing

THE NEXT MORNING Rio was up early, hoping to sneak out of the house before Fran was even awake.

No such luck.

He found her sitting at the kitchen table and, if it wasn't for the change of clothes, he might have thought she'd been there all night. She was hunched over a cup of coffee with Pirate softly nudging her shoulder for attention. Rio wondered whether he ought to say sorry. That was the correct thing to do. The *right* thing. But somehow he couldn't bring himself to do it. The pain and anger in his belly were so loud they blocked any words that wanted to come out of his mouth.

Instead, he crept past the table, hoping she wouldn't notice him.

'Rio? About last night . . .'

'I don't want to talk about it,' he muttered and then without even bothering to turn round, he dashed out of the back door to the sound of Pirate letting out a long, plaintive yowl.

Outside, even the weather matched Rio's mood. The skies were heavy and grey and he couldn't even see where the ocean ended and the clouds began. They were one entwined mass of grey wildness that reared up and down in hard, wrathful gasps.

It was the first time he had seen the ocean angry.

As Rio traipsed along the beach, it felt fitting. His

mother wasn't getting better. She was getting *worse*. And this time he didn't even know when he was going home. It wasn't that he hated it here. He loved the ocean. He loved the whales. He loved being part of the *Spyhopper* crew. But he would have loved it so much *more* if his mother was here with him.

A wave crashed against the shore, spraying Rio with a shower of salty breath and making his eyes sting. He rubbed them crossly. By the time he looked up and could actually see again, he realised he was in the harbour. As if drawn by some magnetic compass to the *Spyhopper* and all she represented. Not just a boat. But a means of *escape*. A place where, if he closed his eyes, he could imagine that everything was well in the world.

Today the boats were buffeted by winds that rattled and shook the masts so they clattered and creaked. There were few fishermen about and even fewer tourists.

But there was the *Spyhopper*, rocking in her mooring, yet solidly and reassuringly present. He half scampered, half ran the remaining distance to the boat before skidding to a halt. Inside the cabin, he could see a warm yellow light.

'Hellloooo!' he called out, his voice swept away by the winds. 'HELLO!'

It was impossible to be heard, so Rio jumped onboard, feeling the coolness of the deck under his bare feet. Even though he had come here plenty of times over the past couple of weeks, he still got that same small thrill each time he stepped on to the boat.

'Marina?' he called and this time the door to the cabin opened and she popped out her head, her blonde mane tousled and wild.

'Rio! I was just about to leave for school,' she exclaimed, widening her eyes when she saw the expression on his face. 'But . . . come on in.'

He followed her into the cabin, which – despite the wind – was snug and warm, and settled down with a whoosh on the bench.

'Birch?' he asked.

'Getting some supplies. When the weather's bad like

this, he uses the time to stock up the boat and make any repairs.'

Marina busied herself at the stove, filling a pan full of milk and making hot chocolate. The noises were comforting and reassuring. Once made, she sat on the bench opposite Rio and slid the hot drink over. 'You know ... if you ever want to talk about things, I'm a good listener,' she said quietly. 'Ocean's promise I wouldn't tell a soul. Not even my dad.'

Rio cupped his hands round the mug. He hadn't spoken about his mother for so long. Even if he knew where to start, the words were trapped somewhere so deep inside him that they had got tangled and caught.

Could he trust Marina? *Really* trust her?

Had she ever let him down? No. Not since the very first moment they'd met, and she'd found the picture of White Beak and handed it back. She'd even believed him about hearing the whales without any real hesitation.

Rio paused. His heart was hammering and his palms

were sticky. He took a deep, shaky breath. Just as he was about to speak, there was a loud crash outside.

'I better go check,' said Marina. 'Something might have fallen over in the wind.'

Suddenly he was alone in the cabin, and the words he had been about to say disappeared. It wasn't long before she returned, letting a gust of cool air into the cabin with her. She sat back down. 'Where were we?'

'We were about to update the database.'

'*We were?*' she asked and then she spotted Rio's set expression. 'Of course we were.'

She slid the laptop out of its cubbyhole and pulled up the Happywhale website. Rio let out a breath, grateful she hadn't pressed him. 'We've just got the other day's sightings to upload.'

Since his time as part of the crew, Rio had got more adept at telling each whale species apart. Although they primarily counted the grey whales, they still made a note of all the different types. The humpback was easy to spot with its white belly and love of slapping its dorsal fin on the surface of the water. However, some whales, like the finback and the minke, looked almost identical, and the only way of telling them apart was from tiny differences in the shape of their flukes.

'So, remember, this is the column where we put the sightings of the individual whales we know more about. That humpback – did you notice how he had some chunks missing from his tail? Looked a bit like fingers, didn't it? Probably a boat propeller,' she said, her brow puckering in disgust.

Rio winced. 'Does that happen a lot?'

She nodded. 'More than people think. That's why Dad never drives the boat too fast and is careful not to get close to any of the whales. Luckily, this one wasn't too badly hurt and, from our point of view, it makes them easy to track.'

She clicked on the screen that showed all the known sightings of the recognisable grey whales. She uploaded her photos and was about to close the laptop when Rio stopped her.

'Shall we check on White Beak?' he asked. 'To see where she is now?'

Marina grinned. 'Good idea!'

With his mum more lost than ever, at least he could track her whale. It wasn't the same. But it was something.

'So, the last sighting was in LA – that's the blue dot there – but that was a few days ago,' Marina said. 'San Diego would usually be where we'd expect to see her next. We often get confirmed sightings when the whales pass by there.' She clicked on a new column and then frowned.

'What is it?'

'No sightings of her in San Diego.'

'Maybe someone missed her?'

'Yes, that's probably it.' She tapped a few keys. 'Let's check Ensenada – that's just over the border in Mexico.'

Rio held his breath as Marina pulled up the data. 'No,' she said. 'Nothing there either.'

'She must have passed and no one saw her,' replied

Rio, something cold and clammy running down his back like ice.

'Maybe,' Marina said, not looking particularly convinced.

'You said yourself you can't count every whale,' Rio retorted. 'Nobody's seen her – that's all.'

'That's true, but . . . but whales like White Beak are always much easier to spot, especially since there's so many whale watchers in that area.' She chewed her lip. 'It's just unusual she hasn't been spotted since LA.'

'Can you check the lagoons?' he asked hurriedly. 'She might have arrived by now.'

Marina nodded unconvincingly. Since the lagoons were essentially very large inland shallow ponds, it was far easier to track the whales in them.

She shook her head. 'No, she's not arrived. It's too soon anyway. She wouldn't have made it there yet.'

'Where is she?' Rio cried. 'She can't just have gone missing!'

At first, he didn't think Marina was going to answer.

The wind howled and rattled the boat, and she rubbed her face wearily.

'The thing is, Rio –' she turned to face him and took a breath – 'sometimes the whales don't make it.'

'W-w-what do you mean?' He swallowed hard, something thick and bulky settling in the pit of his tummy. '*Don't* make it?'

'Bad things happen,' Marina said quietly.

'What kind of things?'

'Like that humpback and the way his tail was all damaged. Sometimes . . . sometimes it's worse than that.'

'How much worse?'

'Ship collisions.' She sighed. 'Ghost nets – they're fishing nets that have been lost or discarded and are just floating around the ocean bed. Plastic, nuclear testing, underground drilling for oil . . . noise pollution.'

Rio had come from the city. He knew all about noise. *But the sea?* Surely below the ocean was the quietest place on earth?

'Lots of ships make the same noise as the whales, and

that interferes with their sense of direction. It's why a lot of them end up stranded on beaches.'

'Like the whale in the museum?' Rio gulped.

'That could have been the reason. No one knows for sure.'

'And White Beak?'

'She could have just gone off course . . . She might have been confused by something or . . .' Marina's voice wobbled in a way Rio had never heard before. 'But if no one spots her soon then . . .'

She closed the laptop and a heavy silence filled the cabin. Not the nice kind of silence they'd shared while lying on the bow end, but the kind of silence that is full of ominous things.

'*White Beak?*'

Something tugged so hard at Rio's insides that he suddenly wanted to cry. *Not this. Not now.* He needed Marina to tell him that there'd been a mistake and White Beak would turn up soon. But she did neither of those things. Instead, she patted his arm clumsily. And the pain returned like a tsunami, tightening its grip round his chest.

'I-I-I need to go,' Rio muttered, disentangling himself from the bench and stumbling towards the door.

Out of the cabin, the sky cast a huge shadow over the water. Wind smacked him in the face. Everything was moving up and down, and he could barely see where the boat ended and land began. He tripped over a coil of rope and with shaky legs, jumped back on to solid ground. It was then the rain started to fall. Not gently but in sharp, icy daggers splintering down from the sky.

'RIO!' Marina jumped off the boat and ran over to him. Rain plastered her hair against her face. 'What's the matter?'

He thought of his mum. Her collection of heart-shaped pebbles, the memory of her coppery hair and finally the way her eyes shone when she played the violin.

'She's probably fine,' Marina said, and it took Rio a second to realise she was talking about White Beak and not his mother.

CHAPTER TWENTY-EIGHT

Whispers on the Wind

OVER THE NEXT few days, Rio scoured the Happywhale database for any sightings of White Beak. He urged Marina to message some of the other whale watchers based further down the coast, in case one of them had seen her and had forgotten to upload their photos.

Nothing came back.

He knew Marina was worried and trying to hide it from him. It wasn't anything she *said*, but then she didn't have to. Rio could hear worry. The anxious tapping of her fingers on the table, the grinding of teeth when she was staring at the computer, and the way she snapped at everyone around her – even her dad.

'Can't we go and look for her?' he asked the pair of them one afternoon. 'If we think she has gone missing?'

Birch shook his head. 'We don't know for certain that she's in trouble yet. It's much more likely she's just swum off course, in which case she'll reroute herself in good time.'

'But what if she *is* in trouble?' urged Rio. 'What if she's out there and needs us?'

'It's not uncommon for grey whales to sometimes turn up late at the lagoons.' Marina bit her lip anxiously. 'She'll arrive soon.'

The trouble was Rio was fed up of waiting. Since the news about his mum, all the old feelings had swept back. And this time not even the ocean could wash them away. The clamp in his chest, the pitter-pattering of his heart, the constant fear that she was going to get even worse. And then what would happen? Because, despite what Fran said about it not being his responsibility to make his mother better, he had a horrible, clawing guilt in the pit of his belly.

Nothing he had done had made a difference.

Not only had Mum gone but so had her whale.

That night, Rio jolted awake. At first, he thought the banging noise was in his dream, but then blearily he realised it was coming from outside. It was the wind blowing in from the ocean and knocking against the pane as if it was trying to find shelter inside the house.

He stripped back the covers and padded barefoot to the window, where he rested his face against the glass and sighed. What if White Beak was in trouble? There might not be any whale hunters in this part of the world, but since being in Ocean Bay he'd learned just how many obstacles whales still had to navigate.

If she *had* got into trouble, what was he meant to do?

Despite the T-shirt confirming he was an official part of the *Spyhopper* whale-watching crew, what did that truly mean? They counted whales. That's all. They weren't superheroes who went out on dangerous whale-rescuing missions every time one failed to show up.

But this wasn't just any whale.

It was White Beak.

'Mum?' he whispered. 'What should I do?'

Rio positioned his feet inside her footsteps and closed his eyes. Trying hard to imagine what she might say. But it was no use. The house was coy and secretive, and any sense of his mother was trapped under the surface. He looked down at the marks and saw them for what they were.

A pair of old, faded footprints. Nothing more. Nothing less.

Suddenly all of Rio's rage rose up within him.

He couldn't even speak to her because she was in that place! All he had was a sketchbook full of whale pictures. That was it. His heart raced treacherously. And all the thoughts he normally kept hidden within himself spiralled outwards. Why couldn't she be like the other mums? Why couldn't she just be *normal*? Because, if she was normal, then he never would have been sent here.

Suddenly the window burst open. Rio wasn't sure if the latch hadn't been shut properly, or if it was just the wind sweeping in off the ocean, delivering messages from far out to sea and howling in his face. But it wasn't the normal sea wind that he heard most nights. This was different. Somewhere, wrapped up in the breeze and whispering something in his ear, he could have sworn he heard his mother's voice calling for him to save her.

He took a short, sharp breath. It was his imagination. That was all. The wind couldn't speak. Rio banged window closed, snapped shut the blind and climbed back into bed.

But it was too late. The wind bumped and shuddered against the house, making the shutters rattle and the

windows scream as the air squeezed its way through. Lying under the covers, Rio could almost feel that the house was shaking, the very foundations shifting somehow.

He rolled over on to his side and found himself looking square in the eye of White Beak. She was staring at Rio. Not just *looking* at him. But pleading with him.

Whether it was because it was the middle of the night and Rio was tired, or because the wind was so powerful it could pass through walls, or whether it really was his mum talking to him, it was as if the wind and the picture of White Beak merged into one. So it was no longer the wind who was speaking but White Beak herself.

And White Beak was telling Rio that it wasn't too late.

CHAPTER TWENTY-NINE

The Plan

'You want to do *what*?'

Even though they were standing at the end of the pier with no one else in sight, Rio grabbed Marina's arm and pulled her closer.

'I want to go and look for White Beak,' he repeated. 'But I need your help.'

Marina narrowed her eyes and gazed at him so hard he almost wanted to take the words back. But then he remembered the feeling of being in the water with the whale – how she had gently nudged him back to the safety of the boat. He straightened his spine.

'And how do you think we can find her?'

'On the database, you said no one had seen White Beak since she passed Los Angeles.'

'That's right. And?'

'And that means we have a search area – from Los Angeles to the lagoons.'

Marina looked carefully at him and then burst into peals of laughter. Which wasn't quite the reaction he'd been hoping for. 'Are you even thinking straight? Do you know how HUGE an area that actually is? It's nearly a thousand miles! You heard my dad. She could be anywhere!'

'I agree it's a large area,' Rio answered, determined not to be put off. 'But that doesn't mean we shouldn't try.'

'We don't even know for sure White Beak is in danger,' she replied. 'Even if she *has* gone off course, she'll probably redirect herself. Dad says it's best to leave nature to it rather than interfere.'

'But what if she's in danger?' Rio retorted. 'What if she's injured? What if she's been hit by a boat?'

'I want to help, I really do,' Marina said, pushing her hands through her hair, exasperated. 'But you don't know how dangerous the ocean is – not once you're out there! It'll be nothing like the boat trips we've taken so far.'

'We can't just do nothing!!' he cried. 'It's not all spreadsheets and filling in columns. This is *real* life!'

'What are you saying?'

'That sometimes real life doesn't go the way you want it to,' he said. 'But that doesn't mean you just give up. It means you do what you can to fight even harder.'

Rio didn't know where those words had come from. They surprised even him. He opened his mouth to take them back but then decided against it.

Marina narrowed her eyes. 'What about my dad?'

'I've thought about this,' he said, gulping. 'We won't tell him either.'

'How can we save White Beak without my dad's help?' She gasped. 'You mean . . . you want us to steal his boat?'

'Not *steal*,' Rio said. 'Borrow. You know how to pilot it, don't you?'

'I've lived on that boat since I was four years old!' Marina replied indignantly. 'Dad says I'm a better skipper than most people his age.'

'Well, there you go then.'

'It's too dangerous!'

'I'm the only one who can hear the grey whales,' he said, fixing his gaze on her. 'Your dad said I'd got the ocean's ear. What if I'm the only one who can help White Beak? To hear if she's in trouble?'

Marina pressed her lips together. It reminded Rio of his grandmother when she was deep in thought. 'I know . . . I know she means something to you. She means something to me too. But looking for a lost whale could mean *weeks* of searching.'

She glanced at her watch. He could tell she was about to walk away, and he'd be no closer to finding White Beak. There was no way Rio could let that happen.

'B-b-but she doesn't *just* mean something to me,' he blurted out.

'What do you mean?'

'You said one time that . . . that I could tell you anything.' He swallowed nervously. 'There is a reason why I need to find her. A very good reason.'

'Well, it would have to be the *best* reason ever.'

Rio took a deep breath for courage. Because, if he wanted Marina's help, then it was time to be completely honest with her.

'It's for . . . it's for my mum.'

She didn't answer but, from her steady gaze upon him, he knew she was listening carefully. 'Go on,' she said softly.

Rio paused. His heart was hammering, and his palms

were sticky. 'She . . . she hasn't been very well.'

Rio waited for the uncomfortable silence or the pitying stare. But instead Marina fished in her pockets and pulled out a tissue, which she pressed into his hand. It was only then he realised he was crying. Not big, ugly tears. But the silent kind that fall secretly down your face.

'Can I trust you?' he asked, after blowing his nose. 'I mean . . . really trust you?'

'Ocean's promise,' Marina said.

He had been holding the story of his mum inside for so long that it had begun to hurt. It was also a story he'd never told anyone before, and he had no idea what to say.

'Start slowly and from the beginning,' Marina said as if reading his mind.

Rio took a deep breath and exhaled slowly.

Then, falteringly, he told her about the time Mum had missed his school Christmas concert because, at the last minute, she'd had a panic attack. The times when he'd come home from school to find nothing in the fridge and her holed up in bed, under the covers. Even the time when they'd gone to the seaside and she'd started crying on the beach in front of everyone. He told Marina lots of other things too. Things he'd never, ever told anyone before. Things that had been hidden for the longest of times.

It was digging under rocks into something dark and shadowy. A place where Rio had hardly dared venture lest he drown. And yet, as each word spilled from his lips, it was as if some huge burden was being lifted from his chest and brought up to the light.

All the time he spoke, he hadn't been able to look at Marina. It was easier to fix his gaze on some distant point on the hazy blue horizon. But now he cast a quick sidelong glance at her face.

'Oh, Rio,' she murmured, and then she threw her arms round him. Rio, who hadn't been hugged like that in a very long time, was startled. She smelled of sea salt, adventure, but most of all of friendship.

'*Please?*' he urged, his voice coming from somewhere very deep within him. 'I have to find her.'

Marina thought for a long time. Then she nodded. 'I'll help you.'

Chapter Thirty

Escape

The plan was simple.

Birch often played pool with some friends on a Friday night. As soon as he left the boat, Marina would call Rio, and then they'd set off. It wouldn't give them much time, but hopefully it would be enough.

Before then, she advised him which items of clothes

to take with him, and with her help he carefully sifted through his belongings.

On the boat, they already had some provisions, including maps, compasses, water, dried food and lots of other things Rio had never even heard of, but which made him realise how unequipped he was for this journey.

'What have *you* got?' Marina asked.

Rio rummaged through his suitcase, pulling out various T-shirts and shorts that she frowned at. 'You'll need something long-sleeved for the boat. It can get cold out there on the water, especially if we're going for a couple days. Sunscreen? Do you have that? Great. Waterproofs? No? Okay, you can take my spare pair.' She narrowed her eyes and looked him up and down. 'We're about the same size.'

Item by item, he put them to one side.

'Now food? Do you have any?'

'Just these,' Rio said.

'*Ginger cookies?*'

The biscuits were unopened but, even so, the scent of them wafted up, bringing his mother so clearly into the room Rio almost expected to turn round and find her standing at his shoulder.

'They're Mum's favourite.'

'Well then,' she said, 'we definitely need them.'

Marina had lent Rio her backpack, and he placed the biscuits carefully on top. He was about to fasten the clasps when the picture of White Beak caught his eye. He picked it up. As the ocean roared approvingly in the background, Rio folded it up and inserted it into one of the pockets.

'Let's take this too.'

Later that same evening, the house was deathly quiet apart from the sound of the ocean breathing in and out. Hanging out in his room, Rio had been checking his phone every few minutes. Nothing so far. Until finally the message flashed up.

Coast is clear!

He pushed back the covers, took a deep breath and crossed his heart for luck. They had left his backpack by the back door, hidden in the shadows at the side of the house. The idea was to exit through the window to avoid passing the living room where Fran was watching the news.

He hadn't told his grandmother about his plan to steal the boat and save White Beak. She'd only tell him that he was wasting his time and no doubt, try to stop him. But Fran was wrong. There *was* something he could do.

As he opened the window, immediately the sea air rushed in with fat, greedy gulps. Having a plan to save a whale was one thing. Putting it into action was another. With the warmth of the bedroom on his back, Rio trembled. Who did he think he was?

But then he thought of White Beak. He could do this. *He had to.* He climbed on to the ledge and then shuffled along to the furthest edge. All he needed to do was reach the next ledge and then shimmy down the drainpipe.

His foot stretched out. Nothing but air. Nothing. And then . . . his toe finally touched the other side.

'Made it!'

Rio half slid, half tumbled down the drainpipe, grazing his knee against the roughness of the wood and bumping his elbow painfully. But finally he was on the sand where he let out a relieved sigh.

The backpack wasn't heavy, but running along the edge of the water in the dark was much harder than it looked. Every so often, a wave would come along and soak him, or his feet would stumble on the loose sand and, once or twice, his ankle completely folded.

After about ten minutes, he had to stop. His chest heaved and his lungs were ready to burst. Then, at a slower pace, he headed towards the bobbing lights of the boat masts. In the blackness of night, all he could hear was the slapping of waves and the eerie creaking of masts.

He was about to head towards the *Spyhopper* when he spotted a shadowy figure only three metres or so away.

'Marina,' he hissed.

She looked around her, startled, before noticing Rio and darting over. 'You're here,' she whispered. 'I wasn't sure if you'd be able to do it.'

Rio could scarcely believe it himself. But he was here. And he was ready.

He glanced at the paper bag she was carrying. 'I was just getting some more food,' she explained. 'Shall we . . . shall we do this?'

Carefully, the pair of them made their way to the jetty where the *Spyhopper* was moored under the gaze of the lighthouse.

The rainbow flag fluttered in the ocean breeze, and, with a small jump, Marina hopped onboard. Rio passed the backpack to her and then followed suit.

'We made it,' she whispered, her eyes glittering in the dark.

'You made *what*?'

A light flickered on and Birch stood on deck, glaring at them.

CHAPTER THIRTY-ONE

Caught

'MARINA?' BIRCH ASKED in a voice as deep as thunder. 'What are you doing?'

'Dad!' Marina stuttered. 'I thought you'd gone out for the evening!'

'I had. But I forgot my wallet so I came back to get it,' he replied. 'But you still haven't answered my question.'

As Marina flapped her hands uselessly by her sides, Rio stepped forward. 'It's my fault,' he said. 'I . . . I wanted to see the ocean at night, and Marina said she'd take me. For an adventure.'

'An *adventure*?' Birch repeated the word slowly, rolling it under his tongue like long-lost treasure. 'Well, you'd best come inside and tell me all about it. And don't forget to bring your luggage with you too.'

With that, he swung open the cabin door. Rio exchanged a quick worried glance with Marina, and then stepped down into the cabin.

With no bright daylight to fill the spaces, there was a completely different feel to the room. Dark and shadowy, a place full of mystery where the faintest whisper of danger hovered in the air.

Guiltily, the pair of them sat down on a cushioned bench.

What do we do now? Rio mouthed to Marina while Birch reached for the jar of hot-chocolate powder.

I don't know! she mouthed back.

234

'The trick with hot chocolate is always in the preparation,' Birch said, striking a match and then lighting the stove. 'That's the same with life. Be ready for anything. Even the unexpected.' Nothing more was said while the milk bubbled, and Birch poured it into his mug, the chocolatey aroma coiling its way round the cabin.

After taking a satisfying gulp, Birch wiped his whiskers and then looked from Marina to Rio and back to his daughter. 'So tell me about this adventure of yours.'

'It was my idea!' Marina announced. 'I said we could pretend to be pirates hunting for missing treasure!'

'Missing *treasure*, you say?' The side of his mouth curled up. 'So . . . nothing whatsoever to do with a missing whale then?'

Marina shook her head vehemently.

Rio sighed. 'It's true. We were going to try to find her.'

Marina swung her head towards him, her jaw tight. 'No, we weren't!'

'There's no point lying,' Rio said, feeling very grown-up all of a sudden. 'Not for something like this.'

Birch nodded his head. 'You, young man, have a wise head on your shoulders.' He took a sip of his drink. 'But . . . there's more, I sense? I know my daughter is persuasive, but even she would have to go some distance to talk someone into going out into the middle of the ocean by themselves.'

'It wasn't Marina who persuaded me,' Rio said quietly. 'It was me who persuaded her.'

Rio had thought Birch might look surprised, that someone like him would have any control over Marina. But instead the older man placed his mug carefully on the table and leaned forward. 'By chance, does this have anything to do with your mother?'

'My m-m-mother?!' said Rio. 'How do you know about her?'

'Your grandmother explained why you'd come here and, more recently, why you're staying a bit longer.'

Rio opened his mouth and then closed it again. *Birch had known all along?*

'Is that why you invited me to join the crew? You felt *sorry* for me?' The words burst out before he could stop them.

This time Birch did look surprised. 'I asked you to join us because you're a brilliant addition,' he said, fixing his gaze on Rio. 'The ocean has taught me many lessons, but the most important one is that there are always plenty of resources deep inside us – and I see that in you. You, son, are more resourceful and stronger than you think.'

He could have been talking about Rio's ability to hear the whales, but Rio sensed that it wasn't the only thing he meant. Birch placed his hand on Rio's. It was rough and warm and steady. And Rio didn't ever want him to let go.

'I know it's an almost impossible task and we might never find her,' Marina said, switching the attention back to their immediate plight, 'but . . . we couldn't just do *nothing*. Rio's right. What if she's in trouble?'

Birch nodded. 'Earlier on today, I checked in with a few of the other whale-watching tours further down the coast, and no one has seen her. Of course, there is a good chance she'll turn up in a couple days and be absolutely fine.'

'But if she isn't?' Rio let the words hang. 'Because if she is lost, then I might be able to help find her.'

The idea that a few weeks ago he would have thought himself capable of finding a fully grown grey whale seemed preposterous. But that was before he'd met Marina. Before he'd joined the *Spyhopper* crew. Before he'd realised he was far more than what he thought he was.

Birch chewed his lip thoughtfully before finally nodding his head.

'You mean we can go?' Marina asked, her eyes lighting up.

Her dad chuckled. 'I didn't say that. You think I'm going to let you two take my boat and head off into the

Pacific Ocean all by yourselves? Rio, your grandmother would kill me. No, I can't allow that.'

Rio's heart sank.

'But,' said Birch, 'what I can do is go with you.'

Chapter Thirty-two

A New Plan

'You'll take us?' Rio asked breathlessly. 'You'll help us find White Beak?'

'Yes,' Birch replied. 'But first I'm going to call your grandmother.'

Before Rio could protest, Birch stepped outside, closing the door firmly behind him. In the sealed hum of the cabin, only the occasional muffled word seeped through.

'Careful . . .'

'Perfectly safe . . .'

'Guardian . . .'

'She'll never agree,' Rio muttered, eyeing the door.

It felt like the fate of White Beak hinged on a single telephone conversation. The cabin wasn't large, but it seemed to shrink even further. After what felt like a lifetime, Birch's voice fell silent. But, rather than come back in, they heard him jump off the boat.

'Where's he gone?' Rio whispered nervously.

'No idea,' Marina whispered back.

The pair of them waited in silence. Apart from the ocean, the only sound was the thrumming of their hearts.

Eventually, the door slowly creaked open and silhouetted against the bright yellow lights of the harbour was Birch. But he wasn't alone. Behind him was another figure. A tall, familiar figure wearing a jumpsuit and a pair of glasses.

'*Fran?*' Rio stood up in shock.

His grandmother stepped into the cabin and peered around before settling her gaze on Rio. His stomach plummeted. No doubt she'd come to take him home. To put an end to the adventure before it had even begun.

'B-b-but what are you doing here?'

She took three long strides and then enveloped Rio in a hug. 'You think I'm going to let my only grandchild take off on the wild ocean without me?'

Rio was surprised to hear the break in her voice. Even more surprising was the corresponding sense of warmth in his own heart. He hugged her tightly before she could pull away. She still had a thing or two to learn about hugs.

'I thought you got seasick?'

'I do,' she said, her face paling. 'But that's not going to stop me from coming with you.'

'I've known your grandmother a long time,' Birch said gently. 'She's been counting whales long before the Happywhale database was even created.'

'You *have*?!'

'You didn't think it was just you who wants to protect them?' she replied, peering at Rio over her glasses. 'Oh no, it runs in the family.'

'But . . . but . . .'

How come Rio had never found any of this out before? It was like he was seeing his grandmother for the first time. Not through the prism of his own pain – because prisms like that are never accurate – but as she truly was.

'I have quite a few contacts, many of whom aren't registered on the site.' She rubbed her hands together in a no-nonsense, school-teacherly way. 'So I suggest before we make haste, we pool our resources. I'll put out a quick call to some of my colleagues to make sure they're on the lookout. Birch – perhaps you can send a message to some of the other whale-watching companies in the area and alert the rest of the network that there's a missing whale? Marina, can you do whatever you young people do on social media? Make some noise? Is that the expression? We might be able to reach some passing boats or even fishing vessels.' Fran paused and turned to Rio. 'And you, young man, have the most important role of all.'

Rio had been wondering what task Fran would assign him.

'You are our ears.'

CHAPTER THIRTY-THREE

Hurry

JUST BEFORE DAWN, the *Spyhopper* approached the harbour walls, beyond which the great ocean lay wreathed in darkness. Fran caught Rio's eye and smiled tentatively. 'Ready?' she asked him.

Rio thought of his mother and of the whale he was trying to rescue, and how the two of them had somehow become one being in his mind.

'Yes,' he said, feeling the words come up from deep inside him. 'I am.'

It would take them most of the day to reach the search zone. But, after about thirty minutes, during which Rio had been resting in the cabin, the engine suddenly cut out. What was happening? Why had they stopped? He scurried to the deck and found Birch and Marina sitting on the portside, bare feet dangling over the edge of the boat.

Birch didn't speak but made space for Rio to sit on the other side of him. As Rio swung down between them, he rubbed his eyes. In the misty early-morning light, the *Spyhopper* felt tiny, an expanse of water stretching in all directions around them with hardly a hint of land.

He was about to speak when he noticed father and daughter had their hands clasped in some kind of prayer.

'Dear ocean friends and creatures of the deep,' Birch murmured, 'we ask that you protect us and guide us safely towards our destination. In return, we promise to look after you, honour you and bestow respect on you at all times.'

Birch kept his eyes closed and then cupped some seawater in his hands and splashed it over his face. Marina followed suit, in a ritual she had obviously performed hundreds of times before, and so Rio reached into the water and did the same. The water was cool and sharp on his face, but it also removed any last hint of sleep. At once, his senses felt alert and poised for the day ahead.

'What was that?' he asked.

'It's something I do each time I set sail on a long journey. An ancient maritime tradition passed on through the generations,' Birch explained. 'Humans often think they're the most powerful things on earth. And quite often we are. But the ocean has been here long before we even arrived and will be here long after we leave. It's always good to remember that.'

Marina pulled out a map and spread it on the deck. 'So, here we are,' she said, jabbing an indistinct point somewhere south off the coast of Ocean Bay. 'We're going to follow the route White Beak would have taken on her way to the lagoons. And the best place to start is here.' She pointed to a coordinate about a hand's-width away.

'Thanks to your grandmother's calls, some of the watchers who live just across the border are combing that area. There's also a couple boats searching around San Diego. So this means our search zone is from just past LA to San Diego.'

'We need to hurry,' Birch said, 'if we want to get there before nightfall.'

Chapter Thirty-four

No Sightings

For the rest of the day, the boat sailed steadily on, stopping only for lunch, which was slightly stale cheese sandwiches and a long, thirsty gulp from a can of Coke.

Although it was hot on deck, Rio and Marina stayed at the bow end the entire time. Marina sat cross-legged with her notebook, while Rio kept his eyes and ears fixed on the horizon. Occasionally, he would check on his grandmother, who mostly stayed below deck where she said her seasickness wasn't so bad. Birch left them all in peace, preferring the solace of his coffee and the feel of the boat under his hands as he navigated the *Spyhopper* against the headwind. And it was this headwind that was making their progress much slower than it should be.

'We'll never get there at this rate!' Rio said, exasperated.

Now and again, they would make radio contact with some of the other boats that were out searching. Each time the radio crackled, his hopes sparked that it was someone confirming they had spotted White Beak, but each time the response was just the same as theirs.

There were no whales in sight.

Apart from the intermittent radio noise, they could have been the last people in the world. The only other sound was the *Spyhopper* scything its way through the water. Hours passed without a single word being uttered, and somehow that felt perfectly normal.

Once or twice, they saw the occasional fishing vessel, and just after lunch a huge cruise liner passed in the distance like a block of flats on water. Rio could just about make out individual balconies, three huge funnels and some kind of elaborate plastic water slide on deck. Even from that distance, the turbulence of the ship's waves caused the *Spyhopper* to rock up and down.

Fran, who had come up on deck for some fresh air, shook her head in disgust. 'Terrible things.'

Marina gazed at it with a worried expression on her face. 'Look at the *size* of it. No wonder so many whales get killed each year by ship collisions.'

In Rio's hand, his binoculars suddenly felt cold and slippery. Before coming here, he had never stopped to think how many threats the whales faced in their day-to-day life. They were the greatest, biggest animals on earth, and, by rights, the ocean should have been theirs – to roam and swim and live in freely. But somehow the seas, like everything else on earth, belonged to humans.

He watched the ship for a long time as it melted into

the distance, heading towards southern California and Mexico, until eventually it was a speck no larger than his thumb and then gone.

The *Spyhopper* motored south as the sun curved across the horizon like the hands on a clock. It was the famous Pacific sunset in all its magnificent glory. Birch turned the engine off, and wordlessly the four of them sat on the boat and drank in the sky.

'Time to stop,' he said. 'Tomorrow is when the search begins.'

Chapter Thirty-five

Sea Storm

That night, Rio was too nervous to sleep. Making sure not to disturb anyone, he crept up on deck. Birch had said they were very nearly in the search zone. Could this mean White Beak was close by?

It was too dark to see anything, but he strained his ears the furthest they would go, hoping against hope that he would pick up the faintest call of the whale. That she might suddenly surface right next to the boat. And that he would see her again and know she was safe.

But, as hard as he listened, there was nothing except the slapping of the waves. Rio let out a sigh. Tomorrow was a new day. Tomorrow they would find her.

Not feeling sleepy, he lay face up on the bench in the bow. With no light pollution, the sky was ablaze with stars, reflecting off the surface of the water like glittering confetti. Gazing upwards, he had the sense he was staring at the beating heart of the universe.

'It's beautiful, isn't it?' Marina whispered, putting her fingers to her lips to indicate he should stay quiet. Then she positioned herself on the opposite bench, lying down as he had done, with her face tilted up to the sky.

Neither of them spoke for the longest time until he heard her sigh and turn towards him. In the darkness, Rio couldn't see much other than the glint of her hair and the flash of her teeth.

'Did you know you're quite similar to a grey

whale?' she said quietly. 'Not how you look obviously. I haven't seen any barnacles on you yet. But, despite all the horrible things the whales have had to get through just to survive, they still keep on swimming. And that's like you.'

Rio had never stopped to compare himself to any animal before, let alone one of the biggest on the planet. But, at the same time, he knew Marina was right. He had faced more in his eleven years than most people his age.

Something loud rumbled in the far distance as if in agreement.

'Sea storm,' Marina said. 'It's probably miles away, but the thunder echoes over the water.'

Rio couldn't see anything. But he could sense it. The air felt charged and heavy as if there was an invisible current electrifying everything – including himself. The hairs on his arms bristled, and his jaw felt tight.

So far, the ocean had been friendly, showing only its best, most beautiful side. But this was a reminder that it

255

wasn't always so kind. Was the ocean angry with *them*? For making such a mess of it?

He let out a long, slow breath, shivering as a stray wave hit the boat, throwing up spray like spittle. But, even though Marina got soaked, she didn't move away and neither did he.

'I'm scared,' he confessed.

Marina looked over at him, and he knew she understood that he wasn't just talking about the storm. He was talking about all his other fears, about White Beak, but most of all about Mum.

'I'm scared too,' she answered. 'Not just about whether we can save White Beak, but whether we can truly save all this.' She swept her hand out to indicate the ocean. 'It feels so huge sometimes.'

'You must never give up hope,' Rio whispered, thinking not just of his mum. 'Not when there's still a chance.'

There was silence. Filled only by the waves. Fierce, pulsing and throbbing.

'My dad says that when you're afraid the best thing to do is look down into the ocean. Apparently, it's a mirror to everything we can be. The first time I did it, all I could see was my reflection.' She paused. 'But I guess that was the whole point.'

Even though it was pitch-black, Rio peered over the edge of the boat anyway. And, in the light of the full moon, he saw himself reflected back. A bigger, bolder version of the boy he'd once been.

It were as if the ocean had crept inside his body and gifted him all its force and power for the adventure ahead. As the storm raged in the far distance, and the sky turned from black to blue to mauve and splintered with lightning, he got a jolt. Because Rio hadn't just come out here to find a missing whale. He had set out to find who he could become.

Chapter Thirty-six

The Search Zone

As soon as dawn broke the following morning, Rio bounded out of bed and ran on deck. Today was the day. Even the air felt different, as if the storm had left behind an aftertaste. Nothing obvious. Just the slightest sense that something had shifted in the atmosphere.

Birch was already awake and gently motored the

Spyhopper further south before cutting the engine. 'This is it,' he said. 'We're here.'

Rio hadn't known what to expect when they reached the search zone, but as he gazed around him it looked no different from where they had been. Just a huge, unmottled expanse of water that could be hiding anything. If White Beak was out here, she could be anywhere.

But the very least they could do was try to find her.

The four of them positioned themselves at various points on the boat. Rio and Marina on the bow. Birch by the wheel on the starboard side. Fran insistent on keeping lookout on the portside.

'I might not be much use, but it's still better than doing nothing,' she said. 'We will all do a visual search. But, Rio, you keep your ears open as well and let us know as soon as you hear anything.'

Rio nodded, his mouth suddenly dry and parched. It was one thing trying to locate whales when you knew they were close by, but another when you were in the middle of the ocean with no land in sight.

Throughout the morning, Birch slowly kept the boat moving back and forth across the search area, while all of them kept a careful eye on the water.

'Can you hear anything?' Marina asked, wiping a hand across her brow.

Rio shook his head. Despite straining his ears all morning, he hadn't heard a single whale.

'It's still early in the day,' he said hopefully. 'She's bound to turn up later.'

As the sun rose to its peak, he listened harder than he ever had in his whole life. Not just for signs of White Beak but for *any* whale that might be out there. But it was no use. The ocean remained frustratingly quiet.

When the others broke for a brief lunch, Rio kept his position on the bow. 'I don't want to miss her,' he said desperately, waving away the offer of food. 'I have to keep concentrating.'

But as the day wore on, no matter how hard he tried to listen for any sign of White Beak, the louder everything else became. It was infuriating. The screeching, squawking gulls, the loud *thwack-thwack* of the water against the hull, even the sound of his own breath, rasping and rattling in his chest.

Yet still Rio didn't move from his position. Not even when the afternoon became hot and heavy. Not even when the surface of the ocean rippled and shimmered in a haze. Not even when he became so thirsty he thought his tongue might stick to the roof of his mouth.

By this time, the sun had started to sink lower in the sky, gently resting her cheek against the surface of the water. Rio's limbs ached. His eyes smarted. His ears hurt. But he had to do this. He *had* to find White Beak.

But it was no use. The harder he listened, the less he heard. Nothing except his frantic thoughts drowning everything else out.

'Rio!' Fran called. 'This isn't working. We need a new action plan.'

With one last lingering look at the quiet ocean, Rio reluctantly joined the others who were standing in dejected silence. Nobody said anything, but they didn't need to. He could feel their disappointment. He had dragged them into the middle of the ocean to find White Beak and he'd failed.

He had let White Beak down.

But most importantly of all, he'd let his mum down.

'You've tried your hardest,' Marina said as if reading his thoughts and patting his arm reassuringly. 'Maybe she's not here?'

'No one has seen her in any of the other search areas either.' Birch took a worried look at the flag, which was flapping briskly in the breeze. 'Wind's picked up.'

Marina frowned and an impenetrable look passed between father and daughter. One that Rio wasn't sure how to interpret, and definitely one he didn't like.

'We have to keep trying,' he pleaded.

And so, despite the increasingly turbulent waves, the four of them carried on searching. By now, Rio couldn't even remember not being on the boat. Couldn't remember what land looked like. Or not having the taste of seawater on his lips or the smell coating his skin. He had left his old self behind onshore and, in his place, somebody else had emerged. As if he had climbed inside a new, tougher skin fashioned out of the sea itself.

But, even with renewed determination, the water remained frustratingly empty. None of the other boats out searching had seen White Beak either.

Where was she?

After an hour more of looking, with nothing to show except for a friendly dolphin, a brightly coloured shoal of fish and ever-worsening weather, Birch stopped the boat. The light was starting to fade, and, in the dusky twilight, everything – including them – had a shadowy, more urgent feel.

Fran insisted that he eat, but Rio chewed his sandwich as if it was made of cardboard. Marina kept clearing her throat, and Birch drummed his fingers on the wheel before finally disappearing below deck.

Rio swallowed. 'What's happening?'

Marina bit her lip, choosing her words carefully. 'Dad

said . . . we'll have to turn back soon. Especially if the weather gets worse.'

'We can't!' Rio cried. 'Not until we find White Beak. I know she's out here somewhere!'

'But . . . but we haven't found her yet,' Marina said. 'And look!' She waved at the grey clouds bunched in the sky and the ominous, writhing water.

'We can't give up! Not now! Not when we've come this far!'

'We can't keep looking forever, Rio,' Marina replied gently. 'Not if there's nothing there.'

He stared furiously at her, scrunched the rest of his sandwich up in his hand and threw it into the sea where the murky depths swallowed it whole.

Birch emerged from the cabin. 'We're turning back,' he said. 'It's too dangerous to continue.'

Rio wanted to protest, but by that point all the anger was packed so tightly in his throat that he could barely even breathe, let alone speak. Raw panic clawed at his insides.

Birch patted his shoulder. 'We tried, Rio. We gave it our best shot. And sometimes that's the most important thing.'

The words were so reminiscent of the kind of thing his mum would say that Rio could almost see her standing at Birch's shoulder.

'One more hour?' he begged. '*Please*, just one more hour?'

'I'm not sure there's any point,' Birch replied. 'I don't think we'll find her. Not now the visibility is so poor.'

Rio was bone tired. Tired not just of body but of soul and spirit. So tired it was tempting to give up. His eyes felt heavy, but the moment he closed them it wasn't dark, comforting sleep he saw. It was the gentlest, kindest face he had ever laid eyes on. The face that had been watching over him his entire time in Ocean Bay. Who had kept him safe in the water. She wasn't just a whale. She was White Beak.

'Let me try!' Rio said desperately. 'Please let me try to find her!'

'*How?*' Marina asked, puzzled. 'She's too far away to hear otherwise you'd have heard her by now. What's changed?'

And then the answer came, as if it had been there all along. 'Because I wasn't listening with my heart.'

Chapter Thirty-seven

Listening

Rio closed his eyes and listened.

At first, there was nothing apart from the beating of his own heart pitter-pattering in his chest. He had never noticed how fast it was before. Jittering and skidding this way and that. Even though his eyes were closed, he could still feel Marina's and Birch's gazes upon him, and he shuffled awkwardly from one foot to the other.

He took a steadying breath and listened harder.

He heard the normal stuff. The creaks and groans of the boat, the drumming of the waves and the flapping of the flag.

And so he dropped deeper. To a place where there were things most humans never stopped to listen to. Had *forgotten* how to listen to.

He heard the creaks and moans not just of the *Spyhopper* – but of all the individually handcrafted planks of wood that made up the hull, the towering oak trees they had come from, and even the rich, fertile soil from which they had been born.

He heard the sky – the whisper of the clouds scudding far overhead and the sacred silence of the blue space above them.

He heard the wind – caressing his face, whispering messages from far afield.

He heard the sea – not just lapping against the boat

but how it breathed in and out as if it was the lungs of the earth.

He heard *inside* the sea – the silvery sparkles of fish, the dolphins, the turtles, the sharks, and he heard the voices of each of them: curious, friendly and often fearful.

He heard the animals at the bottom of the ocean – where mysterious creatures made noises no human ear had ever heard before.

Rio stretched himself to the furthest he could go. To a place where his heart was as open and as full and as alive as it had ever been.

Until, finally, all that was left was him, the boat and the soul of the earth.

It was there that Rio realised something remarkable.

The ocean wasn't just a body of water – something that linked all the land masses together. It was far more formidable than that. It breathed just like he breathed. It got angry just like he got angry. And sometimes it got sad just like he got sad.

The ocean wasn't separate from him. It was *part* of him.

And then he heard something else – something echoey, eerie and beautiful.

The unmistakable sound of a whale.

Rio's eyes snapped open, and to his surprise, the outside world didn't look a single bit changed. But inside his chest, his heart was pumping and roaring and spurting with life.

'That way!' He pointed to the far horizon. 'White Beak is over there!'

Without pause, Birch fired up the engine, and the boat sped across the water. They travelled for over ten minutes, zipping and bumping over the waves, the wind whipping against their faces.

'There!' Marina shouted finally. 'I can see something!'

She pointed frantically at a distant point on the starboard side. Rio squinted his eyes and stared, seeing nothing until gradually a grey shape came into focus.

A whale.

Chapter Thirty-eight

In Trouble

'It might *not* be White Beak,' Birch said cautiously. 'Let's get closer.'

He gently coaxed the boat forward, worry furrowing his forehead. The whale was about one hundred metres away. Rio couldn't see much except for the occasional spurt of water shooting high into the sky.

But, nevertheless, a horrible feeling had climbed inside his body. His fingers tightened on his life jacket, and he watched anxiously.

'Something's wrong.' Marina pressed the binoculars to her face and frowned. 'Look.'

'She's trapped. In some fishing netting.' Birch glanced at the darkening clouds. 'We'll need to be careful.'

'Oh my!' Marina exclaimed, clamping her hand over her mouth. 'The poor thing!'

Because there, in the middle of the Pacific Ocean, was the most terrible sight Rio had ever seen. The grey whale was lying partly on its side, but tangled round it were metres of thick blue rope, wrapped so tightly the whale couldn't move. Worse than that, puddles of blood were pooling round her body.

The boat, now with its engine idling to almost nothing, gently edged closer still, so they were now just a few metres away. Sensing their approach, the whale lifted its nose.

Its *white* nose.

'Rio! You found her!' Marina cried. 'It's White Beak!'

As Rio stared into her face, he knew, for however long he lived on earth, he would never forget this moment.

She was slightly tilted on her left side and her one visible eye stared straight up at him. It was an eye the size of a tennis ball that gazed into the deepest part of him.

'What is it?' Rio asked. 'What's that stuff she's caught in?'

'Blue steel,' said Birch, swearing under his breath. 'It's vicious. Industrial thick rope that fishermen use to weigh down crab and lobster pots on the seabed. Lethal for whales if they get caught up in it – which they often do. The ropes trap them and the more they try to escape the more tangled-up they become.'

'But can't we get her out?' Rio begged.

As if she had heard them, White Beak slapped a fin against the surface of the water. Birch nudged the boat closer still so there was only an arm's-width between them and her. She was three times the size of the boat and so close Rio could hear her breath – rapid and shallow and raw. His heart lurched and he looked away. There was something hugely vulnerable about an animal that size being in such pain.

'She's very weak, aren't you, girl?' said Birch gently as White Beak's fin slowly slipped back into the water. 'Are you going to let us help you?'

'The poor, poor thing. How on earth have we let the world come to this?'

In all the emotion, Rio had forgotten about his grandmother. Her cheeks had gone bright red, and she was staring at the whale with a furious expression on her face.

'We've done this to her.'

Marina leaned over the side of the boat and reached out her hands so they almost touched White Beak but not quite. 'It's okay – we're here to help you.'

'We need backup,' Fran said, squaring her shoulders. 'I'll put a radio call out and see if there are any other boats in the immediate area. How long have we got, Birch?'

Birch shook his head. 'Not long. An hour at most.'

'I'll tell them to hurry.'

While Fran disappeared below deck to make the necessary calls, Marina cooed and whispered to White Beak. Her voice was hoarse and kept breaking.

'It's okay – we're here now,' she murmured. 'We're here to save you.'

Rio steeled himself to take another look. Most of White Beak's body was below the waterline, but her left flank and half of her face were above it. Looking closely, the cords had flayed her skin in several places. 'Can't she get loose?'

Marina shook her head. 'See how tightly she's caught? The more she tries to free herself, the tighter the rope gets. She's so weak she can barely keep herself above water. She'll drown unless we help her.'

Fran surfaced just at that point, eyeing the gathering grey clouds with a worried glance. 'I've radioed out an SOS, but I have no idea how long the nearest boat will take to get here. Hopefully, not long.'

Birch opened a hatch on deck, and pulled out a snorkel mask and an underwater torch. 'For now, I'm just going to take a look. Hold the wheel steady, Marina. Keep the engine in neutral and don't let the boat get too close. Understood?'

Without saying another word, he slipped into the water and was submerged a long time before surfacing and pulling out his mouthpiece. 'It's worse than I feared. Not only are there about five lobster pots snagged up, she's also got a net snared round her tail.'

'A ghost net,' muttered Marina.

Birch pulled himself out of the water and back on deck. He shook his head. 'I'm not sure the other boats will get here in time.'

'We have to free her!' Rio said furiously. 'We can't just sit and wait and do nothing!'

'I agree,' Birch answered. 'But she's extremely weak. And it won't be easy freeing her by myself.'

'But you won't be by yourself,' Marina said. 'We're all here with you!'

'Marina,' Birch replied in a low voice, 'no one is getting in the water but me. She's wounded, and she's distressed, and that makes any wild animal extremely dangerous. One strike of her fin or her tail and you'd be seriously hurt.'

'But she needs us!' Marina gulped, swallowing back her tears. 'I can't just sit here and *watch*!'

'Nor me!' Rio said frantically.

'Me neither,' said Fran in her best teacher's voice. 'But Birch is right – we cannot get into the water. However, that doesn't mean we can't help. I'll get on to the radio again and insist that all boats in the vicinity assist us. I will scream if I need to.' She paused and then switched her gaze to Rio. 'For too long, I've done nothing and beaten myself up about it. It's about time I did something useful.'

Rio gazed up at his grandmother, and an undercurrent of unspoken words flowed between them. The other two knew to stay silent. That whatever was happening was between grandmother and grandson.

Fran knelt down and clasped his shoulders. There was a naked expression on her face that Rio had never seen before, and it was unnerving to see.

'Rio . . . I fear I have let you down your whole life. Not just you but your mother. I'm not sure if you'll ever find it in your heart to forgive me. But I am not going to let you down here.' She paused while she took a deep breath. 'We'll do everything we can to save your whale. I promise you. And that's not just any promise. That's an ocean's promise.'

Then her face crumpled as she pulled Rio to her, and it was the biggest, deepest hug of all. When they finally drew apart, there was a calmness and serenity about her.

'What do you want me to do?' Rio asked.

'You, young man, are going to keep White Beak alive.'

Chapter Thirty-nine

Rescue

Birch had made it clear that no one but him was allowed in the water. Rio was relieved. Under the dusky sky, the sea was almost black and deeper than anything he had known.

'Marina, stay by the side of the boat and pass me the cutters when I say. Rio, your job is to make sure the *Spyhopper* doesn't drift too close to White Beak. If it does, then you put it in reverse. Like this, see? And forwards is here.'

Rio nodded, hoping Birch wouldn't notice how much his hands were shaking.

'Fran will handle the radio and let us know when other boats are approaching. This is not a job we can do alone.'

Birch opened a crate and pulled out cutters, a knife and other equipment. He passed the cutters to Marina. 'I'm going to cut the ropes that are caught round her body first. Then I'll surface, and you can pass me the knife so I can remove some of the lobster pots. And hopefully, by the time I've done that, the other boats will have arrived, and we can free the netting round her tail. Ready?'

Birch looked across at everyone and, one by one, they each gave him a thumbs up, and without wasting another second he disappeared below the water.

From that point on, it was almost like an operating theatre. Birch surfaced, instructed Marina on what he needed, and she deftly handed the correct instrument to him.

While Rio was aware of Birch and Marina, and even his grandmother below deck barking instructions and coordinates to nearby boats, his focus was firmly fixed on White Beak.

This close, he could see all the barnacles down the side of her face, the grey fleshy skin and the one visible eye that gazed unblinkingly at Rio. An eye full of sadness and disappointment and pain.

'I'm sorry, White Beak,' Rio whispered. 'I'm so sorry for everything.'

Birch surfaced, gasping for air. 'She's caught so tight! Is there any sign of the other boats yet?'

Rio shook his head and then watched as Birch disappeared back under the surface. How long this went on, he wasn't sure. Birch disappeared, resurfaced, disappeared and resurfaced so many times he lost count. But, all the time, Rio kept the boat steady and looked into White Beak's eye.

That's how he noticed that the eye had changed. At first, he thought it was the clouds and the way they darkened the water, making it appear grey and metallic. But it wasn't the clouds.

'*White Beak?*' he whispered.

Even though the eye seemed to be looking at him, it was no longer alert but opaque and distant and still.

'WHITE BEAK?' Rio cried. 'WHITE BEAK!'

Something tight and hard coiled inside his chest, wrapping a cold, icy hand round his heart.

'We're losing her!' he yelled desperately, just as a boat finally appeared on the horizon. A small vessel about the same size as the *Spyhopper* with **MARINE RESCUE TEAM** on the hull.

'Thank God,' Fran said, appearing on deck. 'Birch couldn't have done any more by himself.'

The boat pulled up on the other side of White Beak. On deck were two divers, already in professional diving gear.

'I've done the best I can!' Birch shouted over. 'But the tail is completely tangled!'

While the divers dropped into the water and joined Birch, Rio took another panicked look at White Beak. Her eye was closing. Slowly sliding shut against the world.

Closing. Closing. Closing.

'*No!*'

He couldn't lose her! He just couldn't!

Something coursed through his veins like thunder. In front of him, White Beak lay still, her breathing so slow that he wasn't sure if she was in this world or the next.

And, in that moment, Rio knew exactly what he had to do to save her life.

Chapter Forty

Saving White Beak

RIO DIDN'T CARE how deep the water was. He didn't care about the danger. He let go of the steering wheel. He took three steps to the edge of the boat. And without stopping to think he jumped into the water.

His whole body sank under the waves. It was deep and bottomless and dark. And for a horrible second he thought he would never find his way to the surface again, but eventually the life jacket brought him up to the air, spluttering and coughing.

He was dimly aware that Birch had climbed back on to the *Spyhopper* and instructed Marina to hold the wheel and steady the boat. In the background, his grandmother was shouting, although the words sounded blurry and indistinct. Birch snatched hold of the pole he'd used last time to yank Rio out of the water.

'Grab this!' he yelled. 'It's too dangerous to be in there!'

'No!' Rio shouted. 'I'm staying!'

He turned his back to the boat. Now he was face to face with White Beak.

'Hello, White Beak,' he murmured.

Out of pure instinct, he cradled her nose with his arms, resting his face against hers so their eyes were level. Beneath his fingertips, he could sense her life ebbing away breath by breath.

'Don't die!' he whispered. '*Please* don't die!'

There was no distance between them now. Under his cheek, he could feel the soft patch of skin where no barnacles had settled, smell the oily brine of her breath and hear the faintest rumble of her heart. Rio's own heart slowed, in rhythm with hers, so part of him was no longer a boy but had become a whale.

'I've been so afraid,' he said softly. 'About Mum, about life, about everything. But then I found you. And you've been keeping me safe, haven't you? You've been watching over me all this time. Now it's my turn to keep you safe.'

He held her tight.

'I know I can't make Mum better,' he said. 'I think I knew all along, but I had to *try*. I had to do something. You understand that, don't you? You understand I couldn't just do nothing?'

White Beak didn't move. Yet somehow, deep inside, Rio was certain she was listening.

'White Beak? I know you can hear me. Just like I can hear you. I don't know how I can, but it's the greatest gift anyone could have given me,' Rio murmured, tightening his grip round her nose. 'I might not be able to make Mum better, but I *can* do something about you. Not just you but *all* the grey whales. Some battles aren't yours to fight. But there are other battles . . . there are other battles that we can all try to do something about.'

He pulled his cheek back from her skin and swallowed the lump in his throat.

'You're the most amazing animal that's ever lived,' he said. 'I'm just so sorry we haven't looked after you better. But I promise we're going to do everything we can to save you.'

'What's happening?'

He hadn't noticed Marina leaning over the side of the boat, looking pale and anxious, her face wet either with the sea or something else. 'Is she *dead*?'

Rio shook his head and then fixed his attention back on the whale. He cupped her face affectionately – as much as he could cup it. 'I love you,' he whispered. 'Just like my mum loved you. I loved you even before I met you, and I'll keep on loving you. And it's not just me who loves you. It's all of us . . . So please . . . please don't leave us. Not now.'

For a long while, nothing moved, not even the clouds in the sky.

But then White Beak's eyelid fluttered and moved, and her eye slowly opened the tiniest of cracks and Rio could sense something passing, like electricity, between them. Something profound and tremulous. As if she had been jolted back to life.

Her eye prised open even more. No longer opaque but alert.

Not just with intelligence and kindness and compassion and all the things he had seen in it – but with life.

White Beak gazed at him for the longest time, and Rio gazed back. Knowing that there was no difference between them really. Just like there is no difference between any human or animal.

Not deep down.

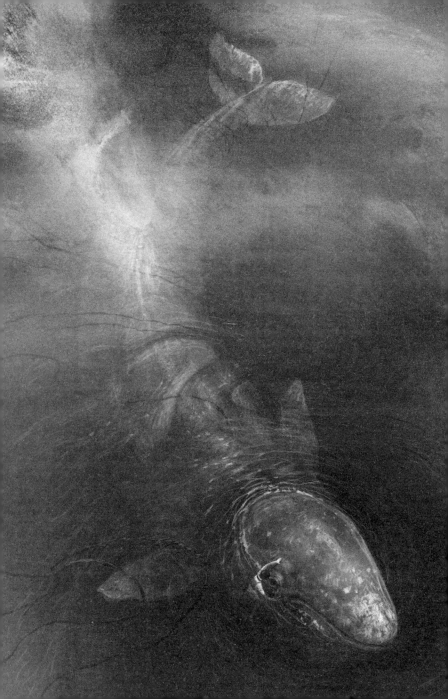

As he cradled her face, the divers burst out of the water with a triumphant yell. 'We've freed her tail!'

'She's moving! Get out of the ocean!' Birch thrust out the pole. 'Now!'

'No!' Rio said firmly. 'I'm staying.'

Birch shook his head. But Rio knew White Beak wouldn't hurt him.

White Beak trembled, and then she nudged Rio gently with the tip of her nose.

'She's telling you something!' Marina called out.

The whale nudged him again. Rio reached out both hands and wrapped himself round her. Resting his cheek on the softness of her face so his eye was level with hers. Looking into her eye, Rio could see right down to the bottom of her soul and beyond. And it was the most beautiful soul he had ever seen.

'You're just saying thank you, aren't you? Because we freed you?' he whispered. 'But you don't need to. It's you who freed me, not the other way around.'

The whale moved softly under his words. 'I'll never

forget you.' Rio kissed her nose. 'Not as long as I live.'

As he said that, a huge spume of water spurted out of her blowhole and caught in the oil of her breath – the biggest and brightest and most magnificent of heart-shaped rainbows.

Then White Beak slowly pulled away and with one last lingering look, she swam off.

CHAPTER FORTY-ONE

Ocean's Promise

THE *SPYHOPPER* STAYED in the area for another half an hour or so, long enough for the crew to help the marine rescue vessel remove the blue steel, the pots and the netting from the water so no other marine animal could get trapped.

Apparently, this was something they did often – freeing

whales, dolphins, porpoises, turtles, who regularly become entangled in ghost nets or fishing debris. Patrolling the ocean so they could remove large discarded or lost pieces of plastic that could be fatal to wildlife.

After it was all cleared, the divers thanked everyone onboard the *Spyhopper* before receiving another call about a dolphin snared up in some netting twenty miles further down the coast. They sped off and suddenly it was just the four of them on the boat.

'Well,' said Fran, looking decidedly queasy, 'you three may be perfectly content out here, but I am most definitely looking forward to being back onshore. Shall we go?'

The *Spyhopper* made good speed. With the wind firmly behind her, she skipped over the waves and by the next morning, they were back in Ocean Bay. Birch gently navigated his way through the harbour, before pulling up alongside the berth. After the silence of the ocean, the sudden hustle and bustle of the quayside was deafening.

Rather than immediately disembark, the four of them sat quietly on deck, each lost in their own thoughts. Rio took a long, yearning glance back out to sea, and it was as if the ocean were reaching out and giving him one final salute.

'She'll be okay?' he asked eventually.

'She'll be sore for a while, but hopefully she'll heal and find her way down to the lagoons where she'll be safe.' Birch turned to him. 'You did a very brave thing out there. Stupid, dangerous – but also very brave.'

'Oh, Dad! What Rio did was *incredible*,' Marina exclaimed, rolling her eyes. 'He saved a whale's life!'

'That's my grandson,' said Fran proudly, putting an arm round him.

'She would have died though, wouldn't she?' Rio said, leaning into his grandmother's embrace. 'If we hadn't found her and cut her free.'

Birch nodded. 'She only had minutes to spare before we got there. It was the right decision to go look for her, Rio. I'm only sorry it took me so long to agree with you.'

Rio shrugged because it wasn't just Birch. There were many grown-ups all round the world who seemed to be waiting for the right moment to do something. Many people who were leaving it too late. Along with all the other whale watchers, at least Birch was trying to make a difference. And sometimes trying was all you could do.

Rio hadn't been able to make his mum better. Whatever he did would never have been enough. He realised that now. But with the net round his heart finally untangled, he might just be able to do something else. Something equally – if not more – important. And this time he wouldn't be alone.

'But she's not the only whale in trouble, is she?' he said. 'She's not the only whale that needs rescuing. There are hundreds, thousands who get killed each year by humankind.'

'What are you saying?' Marina asked, her eyes widening.

'I'm saying,' Rio said, sweeping his arm out to the great blue beyond, 'that there's still a whole ocean to rescue. And we've only just begun.'

Arrival

THE ARRIVALS HALL was busy, loud, as airports always tend to be. But Rio hardly noticed the noise. Standing next to his grandmother, his eyes were glued to the noticeboard.

'What does it say now?' she asked impatiently. 'I left my darn glasses in the car.'

'It's still the same . . . No . . . it's just changed! She's landed!' he said so excitedly he thought his heart would burst out of his chest. 'She's here!'

His grandmother squeezed him tight. Over the past two months, since rescuing White Beak, she had got a lot better at hugs. Not just hugs either but at talking, listening and all the things that were part of being a grandmother. It had made joining the local school so much easier. That and being in the same class as Marina.

After discussion, it was agreed that Rio should stay in California on a more permanent basis and that when his mother was well enough, she would fly out here to live with them. There was an orchestra in LA should she want to join, but if not she'd be surrounded by her family in a place that made her heart smile.

Once the decision had been made, Rio and his grandmother had spent a whole weekend redecorating her old bedroom, and she hadn't even grumbled when he accidentally spilled paint on the floorboards. Instead, she'd just laughed right down to her belly. She laughed a lot these days. It was one of the nicest sounds Rio knew.

That and the sound of the grey whale.

Knowing that Ocean Bay was his new home, it was as if the final shackles had been lifted, and Rio could truly start to live again. Not life as before. But a *new* life.

Days were filled with classes, with ice cream, with activities – all the usual things any eleven-year-old did. But they were also filled with adventure. Boat trips out on the *Spyhopper* as she skipped her way across the ocean.

Not just watching whales. Not just counting them. But *saving* them.

One whale at a time.

While Rio hopped impatiently from foot to foot, his phone pinged with an alert from the Happywhale database. Marina had helped set it up so that every time a sighting or photo of White Beak was uploaded it would let him know.

Rio opened his phone and then gasped. 'Grandma! *Look!*'

She peered closely at the phone. 'Is that . . .?'

Onscreen was a photo of White Beak in the lagoons. She looked healthy and well and happy. But that wasn't it. Swimming alongside her was a tiny grey calf. A mother and her child, together.

'Now isn't that a sight,' Grandma murmured. 'She made it.'

It was in that moment that Rio's heart didn't just smile. It actually somersaulted with happiness. Because walking hesitantly through the arrival gate was someone he recognised. Someone who was wearing a peacock-coloured silk scarf and who carried a violin case in her left hand. Someone who was scanning the crowd intently before resting her gaze on him.

'MUM!'

And then Rio ran forward, spinning his arms like cartwheels before finally throwing himself into his mother's arms.

Author's Note

Something about whales has always fascinated me – perhaps ever since I was in my early twenties and went to Baja, Mexico, with my best friend and saw my first-ever grey whale. It was just a glimmer – a hint of a tail and the long exhalation of breath.

Years later, just before the pandemic, I returned to Baja, this time with my husband with the specific intention of going whale watching as research for this book. We travelled to the marine protected lagoons and spent a life-changing four days out on small skiffs. We must have seen hundreds of grey whales – spectacular breaches, spyhops within metres of the boat and the best sight of all, rainbow hearts suspended in their breath.

We saw males, females and calves – some hanging by the boats for long periods of time, seemingly as fascinated by us as we are by them. There was one moment that will stay with me forever and that was the sight of a grey whale staring up at me from beneath the water. Her gaze pinned upon mine. If you have never seen a whale in the wild, then I hope I have captured some of their wonder and magnificence for you.

Grey whales really are known as 'friendlies' and something about that touched me profoundly. Having twice been hunted to the brink of extinction, they are still incredibly curious about humans and often seem to want to play with us.

Unfortunately, one of the sad facts I learned on my trip was just how much grey whales are in trouble. Like many marine animals, they are bearing the brunt of warming ocean temperatures, plastic pollution, over-fishing, offshore oil and gas development, ship collisions and all the other myriad ways humans seem intent on destroying the natural world. There is actually a real irony in this because whales are one of the best planet savers on Earth and you might even hear them referred to as 'floating trees'. According to the International Monetary Fund, whales can capture and store carbon to the equivalent of thousands of trees. So, it's really in our best interests to do as much as we can to protect them!

While I had to take a few artistic liberties with this story, in particular the timing of the grey whale migration, the Happywhale database mentioned in *The Lost Whale* does exist and thousands of ordinary people, like you and me, do record their sightings. This data is then used by scientists and marine biologists to monitor the impacts of climate change and human impact on the ocean. As Birch says, with knowledge comes the power to change.

If you don't live close to the ocean, the good news is it's not only whales that you can count. There are many similar schemes where you can count birds, butterflies, bees, bats, insects – even fungi! Wherever you live in the world, whether it be the city, the country or the seaside, you can still be a planet superhero. You can check out what's local to you and get involved. It's something you might want to do with your family, your friends or your classmates. And ocean's promise, I'm sure just like Rio and Marina, you'll find monitoring wildlife and being a citizen scientist is a really fun and rewarding thing to do!

In fact, spending time in nature is one of the biggest joys I know. This book was mostly written during the pandemic and it really made me appreciate the outside world and all it has to offer. And for me, my favourite place in the whole world is the ocean. It's always had a massive pull on my heart and is the first place I go whenever I feel in need of a pick-up.

I wish I had known this when I was younger. When I was eighteen, one of my immediate family had a severe breakdown. I can still vividly recall how scared I was at this abrupt and sudden turn of events. Back then, although I had a supportive and caring unit around me, I didn't realise how spending time in nature could ease my worry.

And so, in *The Lost Whale*, I tried to imagine a situation where, unlike myself, Rio had no one to shield him from the worst, and where all the responsibility and weight was on his little shoulders. But luckily, he finds a connection with the ocean and realises being in nature is one of the best healers of all. And although he might not be able to rescue his mother, he does, in a way, end up rescuing himself.

It's no secret that time spent in the natural world improves our health and wellbeing – even if we just spend a few minutes outside a day. But here's the really interesting thing – the more we love and appreciate something, then the more likely we are to do our absolute best to protect it.

As a final note, I know that sometimes the weight of saving the world can feel like a burden on young shoulders. During my school visits I come across wonderful children, like yourself, who care so deeply and yet sometimes feel afraid of what's happening to our planet. But I hope Rio's story shows you the power of what you are capable of, and that by joining forces with other like-minded individuals, we can make a difference, not just to the world around us, but our own inner worlds too.

With love and heart-shaped hope,

Hannah x

Resources and further reading

Here are some of the resources I used in my research that you might find interesting too.

Happywhale database:

The real Happywhale website is slightly different from my version, but the aim remains exactly the same. By encouraging people to become citizen scientists and upload their whale sightings, we can create a world where our oceans are better understood, and more importantly, better protected.

www.happywhale.com/home

Grey whale migration route:

This live interactive map, with all the various observation points dotted along the Pacific coastline, shows the migration route of the grey whale on its journey to and from the lagoons. The fictional town of Ocean Bay would be somewhere between staging posts six and seven.

www.journeynorth.org/tm/gwhaleMigrationRoute_ Map.html

WWF:

You can read more about grey whales here and even watch a video of one of them in the Mexican lagoons.

www.worldwildlife.org/species/gray-whale

Hannah Gold author website:

If you want to check out some photos and videos from my whale-watching trip, then I've shared a few on my website for you. Please excuse all the excited squealing!

www.hannahgold.world

Sightings: The Gray Whales' Mysterious Journey, **Brenda Peterson and Linda Hogan:**

This book is a beautifully written account of the history

and the habitat of grey whales. It's also where I got the name White Beak and the idea for Rio being able to hear them. I bought it during my stay in Mexico, and I wanted to acknowledge it as my inspiration for key parts of my own story.

Mental health resources:

According to Mental Health First Aid England, one in four people suffer from mental health issues, just like Rio's mum. Some of these issues can be quite severe and might need ongoing medication or even hospitalisation. But others are much milder and will seem invisible to anyone else.

If this is you or someone close to you, then the first thing to know is you're not alone. It's natural to feel overwhelmed, sad, scared or anxious sometimes. These are all perfectly normal human emotions. But if these emotions should ever feel too much, then just talking them through with people who care about you can make all the difference.

Just in case you ever need more help, here are a few places you can go to for support.

The BBC has a few useful videos and articles on various aspects of mental health. Just search for Bitesize articles.

Young Minds is a charity based in the UK to support young people who feel like they might be suffering from mental health issues.

www.youngminds.org.uk

Childline is a free phone line for anyone under the age of nineteen to help with any issue you're going through. You can call them, email or chat online.

www.childline.org.uk

Acknowledgements

Writing this book, mostly in lockdown, has been a real journey of discovery and sometimes, just like White Beak, I found myself getting a little lost. Similar to a wild animal, books don't always want to do your bidding.

So, immense thanks to my wonderful editors Harriet Wilson and Erica Sussman for helping me find my way safely to the lagoons, for keeping the faith in the heart of this book and for turning *The Lost Whale* into something I am so very proud of. You really are the kindest, best, most generous of women and I am extraordinarily grateful to have you both on my team.

A book is never a solo effort and I cannot express enough gratitude to the entire team at HarperCollins *Children's Books* in the UK for everything you have done for my Bear and everything you now do for my

Whale. You have made my books look so beautiful that they sometimes take my breath away. To Ann-Janine Murtagh, Nick Lake, Val Braithwaite, Alex Cowan, Jo-Anna Parkinson, Carla Alonzi, Victoria Boodle, Kirsty Bradbury, Geraldine Stroud, Elorine Grant, Kate Clarke, Hannah Marshall, Jasmeet Fyfe, Deborah Wilton, Nicole Linhardt-Rich, Jane Tait, Mary O'Riordan, Sarah Hall, Laure Gysemans and Samantha Stewart. And to Lucy Rogers for jumping onboard this ship and sailing with it to new waters. And likewise, a massive whale-sized thanks to all the team at HarperKids in the US for all your work and effort across the Atlantic.

I have to give an extra special nod to my publicist, Tina Mories, who puts up with my constant questions and works incredibly hard behind the scenes coming up with dazzling ideas. You really are one in a million. And, this provides me with an excuse to give a big bark to Ripley.

Levi Pinfold is not only an utter genius, he also has a knack of creating covers that quite literally blow people away. Your illustrations elevate my words into something unique and beautiful and I am extraordinarily proud to have your name on the front cover.

I am slightly in awe of my amazing agent, Claire Wilson. She's not only exceptionally talented at what she does (all those mysterious agency things!) but is also warm-heartedness and kindness personified. You're always there when I need you and that means a lot. Thank you also to Safae El-Ouahabi.

With *The Last Bear* already out in the world, this also gives me an opportunity to give thanks to all the amazing book bloggers, librarians, fellow authors, reviewers, festival organisers and booksellers who have helped make my debut year so spectacular. Being released during the height of lockdown wasn't ideal, but somehow with your help, you still made my Bear fly. And I am forever in your debt for that.

It's almost impossible to single any one bookseller out as you have all been amazing, but I must give special bear hugs to Nick and Mel at The Rabbit Hole in

Brigg, Helen at Wonderland Bookshop, Ben and Alison at Our Bookshop in Tring and everyone in Waterstones, Peterborough.

Also, extra special thanks to all teachers everywhere for everything you do, and continue to do, to champion new authors and bring a joy of reading to the classroom. You are invaluable and I hope you know that. I cannot single any of you out (for fear of making some huge social *faux pas*) but I hope you know how much you all mean to me.

In terms of navigating my way through various drafts of this book, a collective thank-you to Sharon Hopwood, Polly Crosby, Carlie Sorosiak and Alison Bond for reading early versions and providing such gentle encouragement and guidance.

My trip to the lagoons will stay with me forever and so a big shout-out to my own Whale Pack – Ben, Julianne, Stuart (Sherbet) and Lucie for sharing an experience of a lifetime. We'll make it back there one day with joy in our hearts. A whale-fluke wave to

Sharon, Barbara, Jackson and Rusty and also to Lisa for sending me the details of the Happywhale database. Thanks to the Jasper family – from whom I borrowed the names Rio and Marina. *Gracias* also to Orlando, Andrea and Earnie for making our holiday to Baja so special. We will always love Loreto!

Infinite thanks to all the ocean custodians out there who are doing their best to look after and protect the ocean and to all the whale watchers on the Pacific Coast and around the world – I salute your dedication, commitment and passion. This book is for you.

Hugs to my friends, my family and my ever-supportive parents. It's been so wonderful to share the celebrations with you in the past year or so. Thank you for your constant backing of me, Bear and now Whale!

And of course, to my husband, Chris, who is my biggest champion and cheerleader and who is always by my side on life's adventures. You continue to be the best and in lieu of the ocean, you are the next best thing.

Finally and most importantly, thanks go to my dear readers – I am full of gratitude for your reviews and your roars, your letters and your love. Your enthusiasm genuinely touches my heart and makes my life that much brighter and shinier. I hope you enjoy White Beak, Rio and Marina's story and will take them to your heart and hold them tight. And if you ever see a grey whale in the wild . . . remember to look out for the rainbow!

COMING IN
AUTUMN 2023

FINDING
BEAR

Read on for an exclusive
sneak peek of the first chapter!

CHAPTER ONE

The Photograph

IT WAS EXACTLY seventeen months since April Wood had returned home from Bear Island and she was sitting cross-legged in her back garden listening to the silence. Other people might have said that silence can't make a noise, but April knew differently.

She knew that silence carried all sorts of messages

– especially if you had learned how to listen properly. Besides, she much preferred being outdoors to inside. It was an altogether kinder place.

Particularly these days.

When April and her father had first arrived back from the Arctic, it had been like diving into the deep end of a very cold swimming pool. The constant noise and smog of cars and motorbikes, with their never-ending stench of exhaust, had been the most horrible shock. And *people.* So many people everywhere. Hustling, bustling and jostling every crowded minute of the day.

It had been Dad's decision to hasten the move to the seaside and within a month, they had sold their tall and gloomy city house and found somewhere new near Granny Apples. It wasn't necessarily the kind of house April would have chosen herself. Number Thirty-Four Stirling Road sat in a row of identical modern red-brick houses, each with its own neatly lawned back garden and freshly painted fence. Unlike their old home, or even the wooden cabin on Bear Island, this house was filled with hard, square corners and shiny, gleaming work surfaces. There wasn't even an open fire to toast crumpets on. Instead, it had one of those electric fires with pretend logs that glowed red with the flick of a switch. But Dad seemed happy. In fact, he was the happiest April had seen him in years and, as he kept reminding her, this house was far easier to keep clean.

But it didn't mean she had to stay inside – especially on an evening like this, when the setting sun was streaking the sky with shades of gold and the breeze whispered through the trees like magic.

'It's beautiful,' she said out loud.

That was another thing that had remained with her from the Arctic. The habit of speaking out loud to herself. April didn't consider it strange. Not until others started giving her funny looks.

Thankfully it was a Friday, which meant school was over for the week and she could do exactly as she wanted. She'd only been there a handful of months but still hadn't shaken off the feeling of being the odd one out.

It didn't help that after her presentation about the

plight of the polar bears – the one that had taken *ages* to prepare – most of the class had just yawned. When April had tried to wake them up with her best roar (one she was very proud of) and then demonstrated how she could smell peanut butter from over one mile away, all they'd done was laugh and then make bear noises at her from the back of the class. To make matters even more embarrassing, the teacher had pulled her aside and suggested that perhaps animal impersonations were best kept out of the classroom.

April had tried to explain in her best and politest voice that it *wasn't* an impersonation. That she was trying to inform everyone about the problems in the Arctic – just like Lisé from the Polar Institute had encouraged her to. But her words were wasted. From that moment on, she was known as 'Bear Girl' and, judging from the accompanying sniggers, she wasn't sure it was a compliment.

The article in the local press hadn't helped either. Somehow a local reporter had got wind of April and her father's trip to the Arctic and since it was a slow news week, he'd wanted to tell their story. Dad had been reluctant. But not April. She had seized the opportunity because surely here was a chance to tell everyone about how much the polar bears needed their help. Here was a chance to warn people how quickly the Arctic was melting! But then the article had got lots of facts wrong, including April's own name. As if she were anything like an Alice! And worst of all, rather than saying that *she* had saved Bear, the article implied that the captain of the ship had done all the hard work.

April wasn't looking for brownie points or gold stars or even compliments. All she wanted was for someone to take her seriously. Especially now time was ticking for the planet.

'If I really *was* Bear Girl,' she muttered. 'Then people would be listening! They would be making changes!'

A crow perched on the fence cawed in agreement.

April sighed. It was February and despite a handful of brave daffodils, the air still carried a brisk chill. No doubt Dad would call her in soon – worried she would catch hypothermia or some other life-threatening condition. Ever since they had got back from the Arctic, he constantly worried about her and fretted non-stop that she would fall into some terrible danger. Even now she could see him through the kitchen window searching for her, which meant she only had minutes left.

She carefully took a photograph out from the breast pocket of her blazer. It was the safest place for it, but more importantly, it also meant it was pressed to her heart at all times. It wasn't the kind of photo most people carried in their pockets. It wasn't a photo of a mum or a dad or brothers and sisters or grandmas and grandpas. This was a photo of her and a full-sized male polar bear – huddled together in a tight embrace that would seem incredulous to most people. It was, of course, a photo of her and Bear and it was her most treasured possession. Taken on the quayside in Longyearbyen, Svalbard, the pair of them were silhouetted against the sun, leaning into one other as the flash of the camera caught their final goodbyes. They were pressed so tightly together that it was hard to see where Bear ended and girl began. Even now, April couldn't look at the photo without feeling a horrible tightness in her throat.

'Hello, Bear,' she whispered, hearing the tremble in her voice.

April wasn't sure how long polar bear memories lasted, or even if Bear remembered her at all. Not in the same way she remembered him anyway. She would never ever forget him. Not for as long as she lived. And then for a trillion more years on top of that.

No doubt he was getting on with his new life. The way that Dad said she ought to be getting on with hers. It wasn't like she hadn't *tried*. Every day she did her best to live the kind of life that Dad, Granny Apples and everyone else seemed to expect from her – a perfectly normal human existence. And that might have been enough for some people. But every so often, a memory would surface in April's mind – the tickly sensation of Bear's whiskers on her face, the sudden touch of his wet nose and, most vivid of all, the warm soft chocolate of his eyes and the way his gaze had melted into her own.

'I miss you,' she said quietly, making sure Dad couldn't hear through the open kitchen window. 'I miss you *so* much.'

She didn't expect a reply. The Arctic, after all, was a long way away and April hadn't heard from Bear since their last fateful day together. Bear couldn't write letters or pick up the phone and it was much too far away to hear him roar. But he had, hopefully, found some new polar bear friends – maybe even a mate. Most of all, she hoped he was happy.

'Because that was the whole point of taking you back to Svalbard, wasn't it?' she whispered. 'I just wish . . . I wish I knew that you were all right.'

April breathed in the silence, hoping that somewhere out in the night sky she might receive the answer she longed for. As she strained her ears, she heard the whisper of the silver birch tree, the bark of a dog two streets down, the distant tremor of the sea. But what she couldn't hear was . . .

'APRIL!' Dad flung open the back door and a puddle of warm yellow light spilled out. 'What are you doing out here? You'll catch your death of cold!'

'I'm coming,' she said, reluctantly standing, the evening peace suddenly shattered. She slipped the photo back into her breast pocket and zipped it up tight. Then, as the crow continued to caw, she followed her father inside.